Millionaire Mistress 3

CHLOE'S REVENGE

By Tiphani

Life Changing Books in conjunction with Power Play Media
Published by Life Changing Books
P.O. Box 423 Brandywine, MD 20613

Library of Congress Cataloging-in-Publication Data;

www.lifechangingbooks.net
13 Digit: 978-1934230725
10 Digit: 1934230723

Dedication

I dedicate this book to my mother
Brenda Peggy Joyce Rodriguez Montgomery Ellison
Just because she's the coolest chick I know!

Acknowledgements

"No" is a word on your path to "Yes." Don't give up too soon. Not even if a well meaning parent, relative, friend, or colleague tells you to get a "real job." Your dreams are your real job!"
Joyce Spizer (Author of Rejections of the Written Famous)

My Family
I couldn't ask for better blood to run through my veins.
Wait.
Maybe I could?
Just joking-lol.
Or am I?
Seriously, it was just a joke.
Or was it???-lol

My Friends
You're stuck with me. Deal with it!

My Publisher
You're the best... And all those who worked on my project too.

My Loyal Readers
I'm just a single mother with big dreams. I appreciate you. More than you will ever know. Thanks for allowing me to be creative, in my own world, with my strange, poetic writing style. And Lastly, thanks for making the Mistress Series a hit! Don't forget to also check out my novel, Expensive Taste.

The Roc (Rochester, NY)
• Founded in 1803 by Nathaniel Rochester
• New York's third biggest city
• It's way too cold
• And has no palm trees (which is the only reason I moved)
• 1847 Frederick Douglas founded the abolitionist newspaper The North Star in Rochester
• 1981 A Roc star was born
• 1999 The Roc star (barely) graduated from Rush Henrietta Senior High School
• 2006 The Roc star wrote her first published novel
• 2009 The Roc Star is on to her fourth published novel and counting

Raleigh, NC
• The Capital of North Carolina
• The best place to live if you LOVE college basketball (Go Duke)
• No palm trees, but I'm hoping after a little global warming they'll start growing

Babymamas
Lets raise our standards higher and demand to be married before having ANY MORE CHILDREN!
We're worth it!
And they'll commit…if you will stop giving them some.

Babydaddies
Stop making these kids if you're not going to take care of them…real talk!

And to God who let me lay my head on His shoulder when I could no longer hold it up on my own.
I can always count on Him…and so can you.

Note:
- I had nothing incredibly creative to say to anyone in particular. Guess it's just one of those days. And the reason my acknowledgements were what they were.
- I used some real street names when I was referring to Rochester in the book and then I made up some. There was no real reason for that either. Just kinda felt like it.

Follow Me:
www.TiphaniMontgomery.com
www.Twitter.com/AuthorTiphani
www.FaceBook.com/TiphaniMontgomery
www.lifechangingbooks.net

Tiphani Montgomery

"You don't have to let yourself be terrorized by other people's expectations of you."
-Sue Patton Thoele (Author of The Courage to Be Yourself)

Also By Tiphani

The Millionaire Mistress
Still A Mistress
Expensive Taste

Chapter One
(Chloe)

Fucked up.

Broken.

Left for dead.

But a bad bitch never dies. Not before her time. Not when there are more backs to stab and people to kill. It had been six months since that horrible night in the warehouse where everyone left me for dead. Six torturous months, and my body still wasn't completely healed from the war wounds received that night. Six long months, and this hospital was where I still called home, without any money or the love of my life, Brooklyn, by my side.

Yesterday marked my fifth and last surgery to correct the stomach and small intestinal damage that Bella's bullet was responsible for. Those were the same bullets that were meant to end my life. Bella, just nine years old now, had an enemy for life. The pain that the surgery caused would only last for a few more days, but I just couldn't wait for all of this to be over with.

I had places to go.

People to take off the face of this earth.

And money to make.

For six long months, I remained weak and restless on this piece of shit they called a hospital bed, while I plotted my revenge. I reached over and grabbed the large mirror with the red handle that sat on the food tray. Even though it sat right next to my bed, it took minutes for me to hold it up to my face. Indeed out of fear. Fear of what I would see. Countless times a day, I looked at myself in the mirror, still unsure why I expected to see a different reflection.

It had only been a week since I'd received plastic surgery on my face, and it was still all bandaged up. I looked like a mummy now. But looking like this was much better than the face I was left with. From the knife that had been dug into the right side of my face, to my left ear that had been cut off, and not to mention the burns...I looked like the Elephant Man.

I'd let my hair grow back to the middle of my back in an attempt to hide the deformity of being earless, but wished I had something to cover up my horrible burns just as easily. When Brooklyn left the warehouse, his attempt to set the place on fire succeeded, but failed at the most important task of getting rid of me. I managed to get out with third degree burns to my hands, arms and a small portion of my face. Deep down in my heart I knew that Brooklyn wanted me to live and just had to put on a show for Oshyn. I couldn't wait for the chance to show him that his plan had worked.

I spent every second of every day, every hour of every week, and every month just thinking about how I was going to get each of those muthafuckas back for leaving me scarred for life. Bella, Oshyn and Mye had to die a slow, painful, agonizing death, but Brooklyn would be mine.

I knew he would.

Even though I relived our reunion daily, this day was different. It was the Fourth of July, Oshyn's birthday. One I'd make sure she would never see again. I placed the mirror on my bed and picked up the hospital phone, placing a call to the only place where dudes get things done.

Rochester, New York.

I had my homey, Tuff, looking into Oshyn and Brooklyn's whereabouts, and needed to know if there was any
progress in the search. It had been several weeks since he
started his hood search, and my patience had run its course.

He answered.

On the last ring.

Knew it was me. Wanted me to wait.

"Tuff, why do you insist on making me so damn
angry?"

Little did he know that me being angry was the last
thing he needed.

"Angry. Nobody gives a fuck about your crazy-ass
being angry. Fuck you, Chloe! And didn't I tell you that I
would call you when I got the information?"

I took a deep breath and weighed my options of cursing him out, but quickly realized that wouldn't do me any
good. I wasn't in a position to make too many demands, so
for now I had to comply. Later, I vowed to myself, he would
pay.

"Well, when the fuck will you know?" I asked anxiously.

This was as nice as I could be.

"All I know for now is that they're living in another
country."

In another country, I repeated to myself, as I wondered where they could've moved to. Ever since Oshyn
heard the horror story of her mother going into labor on a
cruise ship, she never really trusted foreign travel, and always wanted to stay in the states just in case things went
wrong. But I could never fully understand why...especially
since they were all lies.

Her mother wasn't really her mother, and the stories
Roslyn made up were concocted only to cushion the blow of
the truth of how she was conceived, which was by rape. I
couldn't help but to laugh, as I thought of how meaningless
Oshyn was even at the beginning of her life. Conceived out
of hate, she was never wanted. But killed out of hate would

be my job.

"When will you know?" I asked Tuff again in my deep, kick-ass voice.

"I just haven't pinpointed where they are yet. I should know by next week at the latest."

"Next week? Muthafucka, we ain't working on black people time! I need this information now!" I tried being nice to his faggot-ass, but dudes like him only understood being talked down to. He didn't deserve respect. "I knew that your whack-ass couldn't get something like this done."

His breathing pattern shortened.

Yet got heavier.

I could sense that I was pissing him off, and I was pleased at how easy it was to throw him off track. He was a man that hadn't mastered his emotions, and I knew that I would be able to take him off his game at the drop of a dime. *This is going to be too easy*, I thought.

"Never send an incompetent little fucking boy to do a grown man's job!" Disgust filled my voice.

His breathing patterns now resembled an asthmatic wheezing. I was sure that I had struck a nerve.

"Yo, you lucky you not in front of me right now or I would…"

"Or you would what?" I butted in, not allowing him to finish his sentence. "Kill me?"

I laughed.

Hard.

It took all the strength that I had in me to calm myself down. I couldn't remember there ever being a time when I just sat back and allowed a man to talk to me any kind of way and didn't put him in his place at that very moment. But I realized that things had to be handled very differently this time around. If I wanted to win this war I had to lay siege very carefully with patience and precision. Two of the very things I knew nothing about. Two of the very things I'd had to learn quickly while in recovery.

"Like I said bitch," he continued, unfazed by my laughter, "you lucky." He paused for a few seconds. "Here's a phone number," he said nastily before rattling off thirteen , long numbers. "Try that for now, but I want an extra two hundred if it works."

"Yeah…whatever, nigga. Just call me when your dumb-ass got my information!"

I hung up on him before my malicious words took control and I ruined everything. Butterflies flew around in my stomach, and my mouth began to water because I knew that the time was near. I could taste it. By this time next week I would get my revenge. Bandages or not, I'm on the first thing smoking when Tuff called me with their location.

Chapter Two
(Oshyn)

"Happy birthday to you, happy birthday to you, happy birthday dear Oshyn…happy birthday to you!"

Rich.

Dark.

Pecan.

That was the color of my kitchen table that I sat at with a smile painted on my face. Brooklyn and Bella serenaded me with the happy birthday song, while Mye Storie, oblivious as to what was taking place, just smiled and slobbered, seemingly hypnotized by the flames of the twenty-six red, white and blue candles. The sweet smell of my homemade buttermilk strawberry flag cake made all of their mouths water as they waited anxiously for me to blow them out.

"Make a wish!" Bella demanded.

However, I just sat there in the midst of what seemed like hundreds of balloons.

Frozen.

Unable to dream of a better life, where my whole family was alive and together again. A life where my Aunt Mahogany and my mother shared sisterly love. A life where me and Chloe did the same. A life where my first born son and my best friend were back and alive again. And my grand-mother's heart didn't fail her because of all the pain this family had caused her.

I just sat there.

Not knowing what to wish for.

Not quite knowing if wishes still came true.

"Hello? Earth to mother, is anybody home?" Bella asked sarcastically.

She was grown as hell to be just almost ten, and insisted on calling me her mom. Even though her fair skin, which was decorated with freckles and her green eyes, both made her look like the spitting image of her mom, Apples. I could tell that she was slowly forgetting who her mother was. I did everything in my power to make her remember, but it was as if she didn't want to. I had concluded that maybe it just hurt too much. Maybe she wanted to pretend as if the last two years of her life never existed. As we all did. As I desperately tried to do constantly.

"Mom!" she said, in slow motion.

Her neon green fingernails swayed in front of my face in an attempt to mimic a handicapped person. As if I needed special communication. She straightened the dumb crystal tiara that I was forced to wear back onto the center of my head, and then stood in front of me with her hands crossed over her chest. A chest that had grown breasts the size of mosquito bites. I expected her period to come within a year or so, which was another problem that I could seriously do without.

I felt my husband staring at me as he sat off to the side, holding our son on his lap. I guess he couldn't take anymore of my non-responsiveness when he asked, "Baby, we're waiting on you to make a wish. What's wrong?"

I lowered my head, as I felt the tears heading to the surface. I kept my long silky black hair in the way, because it acted as curtains which, for the moment, hid my soul. I couldn't answer Brooklyn either.

So, I sat in the kitchen of our large four bedroom, two

8

and a half bathroom villa, inhaling the scent of smoked bar-
b-cue, cake, and ocean water. The true scents of Independ-
ence Day, minus the fireworks since we no longer lived in the
land of the brave.

Saint Tropez was now the place I called home. Lo-
cated in southern France on the French Riviera, my new
home was known best for its famous and wealthy guests.
The weather was what you would expect of a Mediterranean
climate; scorching hot summer days, relieved by refreshing
evening breezes, and an incredibly mild winter. There was
no place I'd rather be, and often kicked myself for not thinking about moving here sooner.

I eventually broke out of my trance, and looked up
slowly like Oprah Winfrey's character, Ms Sophia did at the
dinner table before she made her big speech. I had no idea
who didn't like the movie, *The Color Purple*. It was my fa-
vorite.

"Ummmm…," was all I could muster up before the
phone rang for the second time today.

Brooklyn looked at the phone and then back at me,
and said, "Just forget it. Finish what you were saying."

"No…answer it," I suggested, wiping my tears away. I
was no longer in the mood to make my big speech. There
was something more important that needed to be taken care
of.

"Baby, it's probably just my job calling. J'eun was
supposed to cover for me today, but he never showed up.
This is a holiday. You know the Fourth is the busiest time of
the year. They probably just want me to come in because he
didn't." Brooklyn turned his back to me. Probably didn't want
me to see him lie to my face. "I'm not going in today, so they
can forget it," he ended, just before the phone stopped ringing.

Chateau de la Messardiere, one of St. Tropez's most
popular resorts, was where Brooklyn worked as a bartender.
Although it sounded like he made meager wages, we lived
more than comfortably in a three hundred and twenty thou-

sand dollar home that had a great ocean view. The resort was a hot draw for celebrities, models and moguls, not to mention July being the island's busiest month, but I wasn't buying it.

"No, that's not it," I said calmly. I flung my hair back behind my ears to get the strands out of my face. I wanted him to watch my face wrinkle up, showing him that I meant business. "Two times today that phone has rung, and both times all I heard was someone breathing on the other end before hanging up."

I knew in my heart that something wasn't right, but he was doing everything in his power to convince me otherwise.

The phone rang again.

And then again.

And then again.

And then it stopped.

"There, the ringing finally stopped. Now, please blow out those candles before the wax melts into the cake and we can't eat it!" Brooklyn said impatiently, as his six foot four frame towered in front of me.

He handed his son, who was a spitting image of him, to Bella and then turned his attention back to me, lowering himself to be able to place his lips on my forehead, and then again on my lips.

"Ewww, get a room," Bella snarled as she turned away, trying to rid herself from the torture of witnessing true love at its finest.

I looked into his gray eyes and suddenly remembered the first time we fell in love, when the worries of the world hadn't yet been placed on our shoulders. Before he betrayed my trust and I forgave him of his sins.

He brought me back to the present moment as he smiled at me, like he always did, showing off his trademark gap that made me crumble. The wife beater that he had on revealed a body that he'd worked so hard at perfecting, and the tattoos on his arm that still read: **BROOKLYN'S OSHYN** and **RIP MICAH**.

The phone rang again, snapping me from my thoughts of our past, and I found myself staring at Brooklyn, no longer in admiration, but in anger. Telling him through my eyes that he better pick up the phone this time. Thank God he listened.

"Hello? Hello?" He paused and then let his eyes meet mine. "Hello!" he said once more before hanging up.

"Guess that wasn't your job after all, was it?"

I was being funny, but no one was in a laughing mood. My birthday had been ruined by the anonymous serial caller. I wasn't sure why he didn't want to admit that something more sinister was happening, but I knew.

"Bella, take Mye upstairs," Brooklyn instructed.

"But what about the cake?" she whined.

"What did I say?"

His tone got hard.

Fatherly.

"What's wrong with you?" she screamed at me angrily. "We're finally a normal family again! Why are you ruining everything?"

Brooklyn, not believing that she disregarded his instruction and was now talking reckless to me, lowered his eyebrows, increased the boom in his voice, and asked her, "What did you say?"

"I just want to know what's wrong with her." A tear rolled down Bella's cheek as she looked at me, expecting an answer.

An answer I couldn't give.

Because normal didn't exist in my world anymore.

Because I was unsure of everything.

"Look at her," Bella continued. "Her expression even looks funny."

I slowly turned my head to the right and stared at the antique French mirror that sat on the dining room wall, trying to see what stared back at me. I noticed that my eyes were glassy.

Red.

11

Confused.

I rubbed my slightly chapped lips together, exposing the one dimple in my cheek, and let the tears that began to form freely fall. I still looked like the same ole Oshyn, but I was tired.

Very tired.

"Bella, get your ass up those damn stairs and don't make me say it again," Brooklyn warned. Realizing that the next time he yelled would most likely be followed by his big hand, she got up with Mye hanging off her side and rolled her eyes as she carried the one year old along with her.

As if he aggravated her.

Like she did us on a regular basis.

"Oshyn," Brooklyn said, before finally blowing out the candles himself. After that he took a seat by my side. "Talk to me. What is all of this about? Your whole attitude seems like it's coming out of nowhere. Everything was cool yesterday, last week, last month. What happened today?"

He was right.

I had changed. Drastically.

I had been fine this whole time, and was quite surprised as to how easy the transition to the island from the states had been. The culture shock, and the fact that none of us spoke French, were a bit different, but it didn't affect us too much. We weren't a mingling family. I home schooled Bella, and we never did too much socializing with the natives. We had each other, and clung to that as if our lives depended on it, because it did.

We all coped the best we knew how since the tragedy. While Bella pretended like nothing ever happened, Brooklyn found ways to bring it up every chance he got. As if he were a detective trying to find a missing piece of his life. Like the night six months ago when he lost his memory, which was never fully restored. I always tell him to count himself blessed, but he didn't see it that way. He just wished he could remember what happened to him, while I wished I had his gift to forget.

12

"Oshyn," Brooklyn stated.

"What? Just leave me alone!" I fired back.

"Who are you talking to?" he raised his voice, before realizing that I wasn't one of the kids.

I was glad he stopped himself when he did because that was going to be another argument I didn't feel like having at the moment.

"Leave me alone. Seriously, just leave me alone!"

"No, I'll never leave you alone. Baby, everything is over, and you have nothing to worry about. Chloe is dead, remember? I'm back for good. I'm never going anywhere. I got you. You're safe." His New York accent melted me. And his strong arms were now extended for me to climb into.

"I just wish that I could've seen them bury her so that I could be sure, you know?"

Brooklyn shook his head. "Baby, that bitch is dead, believe me. I was the last one to see her. There was no way she could've survived that fire."

I didn't believe him, and at that moment it was something that I couldn't explain, but fear had come back over my life.

"Relax," he said calmly, as he leaned in and lubricated my lips with his. The sweet and spicy taste of his homemade bar-b-cue sauce let me know that he had been secretly meddling in the food.

"Why are you eating the food while everyone else is starving?" I asked, while playfully shoving him off of me.

"Please, you, Bella and Mye could afford to skip a few meals." He grabbed a small roll that had developed on my stomach and stuck out from my black Gucci tank top, right before I hit him on his shoulder. I was trying to get him away from me while he pulled me closer. "I love it though," he continued. "I love all this juiciness."

He then grabbed my butt, which was covered in a Gucci khaki skirt, and had noticeably spread from a size six to a size eight.

He was right.

Me, Bella and Mye had put on several pounds since we moved here six months ago. I couldn't tell if it was the stress, or the mere fact that Brooklyn cooked everyday, or a combination of both, but we were thick.

He grabbed the hand that held my princess cut, eleven carat wedding ring and said, "See, if you gain any more weight, your finger is going to be suffocated and it'll have to be cut off to get the ring off!"

He was right again. My big-ass wedding band had a serious death grip on my ring finger, and I knew I'd have to either lose some weight or get another ring. I'd be pushing for the latter.

"Come here. I have a birthday gift for you," Brooklyn stated.

"Babe, I told you not to worry about getting me anything. I don't need a gift. You're everything I need."

"Ah, shut up and come on."

He forced me up and led me by the hand to our first floor master bedroom, which had the distinct shape of a t-shaped suite and an extended view of the sea. He placed me on our oversized king bed and then walked back to the door to lock it. This was obviously a grown up gift that he didn't want anyone else to see.

He wasted no time undressing me, starting with my wife beater and bra, continuing non-stop to my khaki skirt and matching panties. As I lay naked on all one thousand counts of our white sheets, I watched him as he pulled his wife beater over his head and his Armani dark denim jeans off of his sexy dark legs. The tables had turned, and he was now standing before me in his well endowed birthday suit.

I spread open my legs, grabbed his flawlessly wavy brush-cut head and pulled it toward my pussy.

Because that's where he wanted to be.

Because that's where I wanted him to be.

My pussy began to throb at the slight breeze that passed by it, which came from the air flowing from his mouth.

14

And then he kissed it.

French kissed it.

He made out with my pussy as if it had been an eternity since the last time he saw it, making sure to focus on my clit because that was how I liked it, and he knew it. I arched my back slightly, trying to maintain my composure while he sucked on it.

"Oh my God," were the words I allowed to slither out of my mouth, as I found myself in heaven with the man of my dreams.

My soul mate.

My husband.

"What are you trying to do to me?"

I moaned, slightly losing control of the arch in my back and violently jerking, trying to keep myself from cumming while he had me pinned down. He slurped, sucked and spit in it until I just couldn't take it anymore.

"You...have...to...stop...now...please...let...go...don't...want...to...cum...now." But my cries fell on death ears.

His hold was too tight on me and I couldn't loosen myself from his grip. My skin began to glow as my sweat glands sprung into action, and my nipples hardened like rocks.

"Pleaseeeee Brooklyn, stop. Come...up...here," I begged. "Kiss me."

But he wouldn't listen. Instead, he went the opposite way, stopping the love making of my pussy to extend the same courtesy to my French manicured toes. He took his tongue and ran it smoothly through each toe, taking his time to give each little piggy his undivided attention.

"Shit!" was what I romantically said, as I bit my lower lip and laid my head back to stare at our high ceiling. "Shit, shit, shit!"

Who would've thought that toes could feel so good, I wondered, as he continued with his journey. Finally, he stopped on the last toe and moved his thick, chocolate body on top of mine.

As his face brushed up against mine, I allowed my

15

lips to softly kiss his cheeks. He was perfect in every way, with skin as soft and smooth as Mye Stories' butt. He moved his lips to mine and kissed me softly.

Gently.

Like he was in love with me and he was happy that I was his wife. He stuck his soft, sweet tongue out and I took it into my mouth hungrily. My head got to bobbing back and forth as I stroked his tongue just as I had done his magic stick on plenty of occasions.

And then he kissed me hard.

Passionately.

For a long time.

For what seemed like eternity. And I loved every minute of it. Brooklyn and I had sex everyday, and we were so attracted to each other that each time felt like the first. He wanted me as much as I wanted him.

I got wetter as I felt his big, black dick getting harder and expanding on my leg. It began to throb and jump as it got near my bottomless pit. He was ready and so was I.

Brooklyn put it in.

I gasped.

And I let out a breath of air as I welcomed him into his home.

"Happy birthday, baby," he whispered, as he rocked back and forth on top of me. I wrapped my arms around his back and my legs around his butt as he dug deeper into my pussy.

"Ah, Daddy…oh my God, please," was all I could muster, as I dug my head into his shoulder as he relentlessly pounded my pussy out.

With each wild stroke, he kissed my face, and then my neck, and then my breasts, making sure to take his time nibbling on both nipples, giving them both the same amount of time. I threw my pussy at him with each thrust he gave and came before I wanted to.

"Jesus, that felt so good!" I said, panting heavily.

"Oh yeah?" he murmured, as he kept pumping.

He was ready for round two, and I could tell that he had built up lots of energy for this one. I let my hands wander around his body before running my fingers through the crack of his butt and landing them on his hole.

"What the fuck are you doing?" he asked, before pulling himself off of me.

He had an obvious attitude.

"I was just playing around, baby. Come back."

But he wouldn't come back. He seemed to be past angry at what I had just done. Although I had never tried anything like that with him before, I made a mental note to never do that shit again.

"I'm sorry," I pleaded, this time with my bottom lip poked out. "I'll never do that again, I pinky promise."

I extended my pinky out as my binding contract and waited, while he just stared at me, still visibly angry. Like he had been violated and this had happened before.

Like I wasn't his wife.

I got off my back and straddled him. His dick had gone a little limp, but I knew that I could get it back up in no time. I rubbed my pussy on it while I kissed him on his neck.

And then his ears.

And then his lips.

I felt the magic wand working as it rose back up to the occasion, and before he changed his mind, I jumped on it and rode it like I was on a wild bull in the wild, wild west.

He had forgiven me.

It didn't take long for my bull to cum, and when he did, he yelled out so loud I just knew the children were going to hear him. I felt every inch of his thousands of babies swim up my stream, trying to hibernate in eggs that would never accept them. My birth control pills would never allow that. More kids were no longer in my future. We lay holding each other in our own sweat, and stayed there until both of our breathing patterns calmed a bit.

"I love you," I let him know after I kissed his wet and salty forehead.

"I love you too."

"I want to ask you something."

"What's up?"

"Why did you get so angry when I touched you there?" I asked in a soft tone.

I felt his body tense back up.

Like a nerve had been struck.

"I'm a man. Men shouldn't be touched there. It's just not right, so don't do that shit again," he demanded.

"Get your panties out of a bunch; I was just playing with you."

I wanted to tell him that he had been raped and just couldn't remember, but I left it alone. Instead I rushed to get on top of him again, but the phone rang. Brooklyn reached over and picked it up with speed before I could.

"Hello? Who is this?" he screamed, taking his hostility against me out on the caller.

And then with the phone still glued to his ear, he paused, looked me in my eyes, only to quickly dart them back at the ground. He avoided any kind of eye contact with me. Avoided any kind of questions I was going to have. He fidgeted with the phone for just a little while longer…just listening before hanging it up.

"Tomorrow we're going to get this number changed," he said to me. And then the phone started ringing again. "It's probably just some dumb kids playing on the phone."

"Are you sure? Isn't there some way we can get the calls traced?"

This was one of the rare moments when I missed the simpler things in life, such as caller ID. For whatever reason, we didn't have it, and in all actuality we never thought we were going to need it. Guess we assumed that all our troubles were behind us, but I was slowly beginning to think that we were wrong. At this point, I had gotten hyped like I was in a Lifetime movie, trying to think of any solution that would solve this mystery.

"No, Oshyn. Calm down. Just relax. You're overreacting, baby. Just chill out and I'll take care of changing our phone number first thing in the morning."

"But I know it was her! It was Chloe calling here! What did she say to you?"

The thought of getting my husband to believe me would have made me feel a little better, but my concerns fell on deaf ears. He looked at me with the same stare that I had gotten from him all day.

Like I was crazy.

"Oshyn, for the millionth time…chill out. That wasn't Chloe!"

Chapter Three
(Chloe)

"There you go!" my nurse, Fay, said after unraveling the last bandage from off my face.

It had been almost two weeks since my plastic surgery, and I was relieved to finally have all that shit off of me. Fay handed me the red mirror that never seemed to be too far from my side and held it up to the ride side of my face.

"You look beautiful," she said.

I, however, stared at my face in disgust as soon as I caught a glimpse of the final results.

"You must've been paid to say that stupid shit. Look at me!" I dared her, hardly able to commit to the same task myself.

The cuts and burns didn't seem to have gone away completely, but rather took on a more plastic approach.

It had the texture of rubber.

Not skin.

Accompanied with some of *Flavor of Love's*, Delicious' big-ass keloids, I looked like a damn fool. My ear that was cut off was now replaced with a decoy that looked exactly like a decoy.

The nurse, who watched quietly as I examined myself

in disgust, took a few steps back to my side, put the mirror down and said, "You don't look that bad."

"Fuck you, bitch!" I snapped.

My nurse was drop dead gorgeous.

The way I used to look.

Dark chocolate was the color that adorned her skin, and her double-D breasts looked to have been done by the finest plastic surgeon in town. Her long wavy weave fell down to her tailbone, and she had dimples that reminded you of a Cover Girl model. She was high maintenance, someone who should've been amongst the A-List stars as opposed to the D-List diseased. I felt like she was taunting me.

I could feel the veins popping out of my neck, as I tried with everything I had not to slap her. She was much prettier than I was right now, and I knew that she was taunting me. She was trying to take advantage of the fact that for a moment she looked better than I did. She was lucky I didn't have a weapon on me because those would've been the last words she ever spoke.

But I also noticed something else.

My face didn't move how it normally did once she took the bandages off. My eyes didn't close all the way either, and they seemed to well up with tears, despite the fact that I wasn't crying. Numbness filled my mouth area, and even though the nurse was getting on my last nerve, my face re-mained emotionless.

"My face," I said to her, touching it lightly, trying to cure it myself. "Something is wrong with my face! I can't feel it…something went wrong!"

I became frantic; couldn't afford for anything else to go wrong. I had to leave as soon as possible, and was afraid that was no longer going to happen.

"Well, Chloe, of all the cranial nerves, the facial nerve is most susceptible to injury. You encountered a lot of trauma. And remember, we warned you that it was a possi-bility that your face could be damaged even further with this cosmetic surgery."

"I don't even know why I'm wasting my time with you. You're just some retarded-ass nurse. Talking to you is like speaking to a child. I want to speak with a real doctor. Now!"

"Excuse me?" she asked.

Her facial features worked just fine, because I watched the wrinkles on her forehead curl up, showing the disdain she had for me.

"You heard what I said. Get me a muthafucka in here who knows what the fuck they're doing!"

"What's going on in here? Chloe, what's wrong?"

Tommy.

My security.

An old man who'd also been a patient of the hospital longer than he had hoped. An old man, who was responsible for paying all the costs, including my stay here and the plastic surgery. He was a seventy-two year old albino man who was battling some form of cancer, yet would never tell me which one it was. I really didn't care either way.

"My face!" I cried, trying to be dramatic, and realizing that my face didn't line up with my theatrics. Instead of looking sad, I had a pitiful blank stare that said absolutely nothing. "They messed up everything. My face is ruined forever! I'm going to sue all you bastards," I warned Fay.

Those were the words that got her out of my room without saying another word. Hopefully my real doctor was on the way in.

"But, sweetheart, you look beautiful," Tommy said sincerely.

His words weren't comforting in the least. He was a dying old man who wanted companionship and would say anything to get it. He moved in closer toward me, and as he did, I smelled his stale scent of oldness breeze by my nostrils, making me wish that my smelling senses had disappeared as well.

Old man Tommy was unattractive, tall, and so skinny that he was beginning to resemble a skeleton. If I could've guessed it, I'd say that he only weighed a little over one hundred and ten pounds. The skin on his face had begun to droop down, and his eyes had started to sink in. The chemo had taken its toll on his body, and from the looks of it, he wasn't going to last too much longer.

The red dingy Kango hat he always wore seemed to boost his self-esteem because he had it on every time I saw him. I could tell that it was something he wore when he was younger, and now since the days of death seemed to be fastly approaching, he wanted to keep what youth he had left.

Let Tommy tell it, it was love at first sight. The night I was rushed into the emergency room from the warehouse, was the night when he had decided to take his own life. It was also the night when his will to live returned, and he made a vow to take care of me for the rest of his life. I could give a rat's ass about his story. As long as he felt the need to take care of me, we would be okay. While I continued to cry a tearless cry, my doctor knocked on the door that had been left open by Tommy.

"Hey Chloe," Dr. Kroon said, as he made his way over to me. He took his fingers and softly went over his work. "Yup, things seem like they went really well. I'm extremely happy with the progress."

"What the fuck! Am I in the twilight zone? I can't feel my face, the scars look like they've been glazed over with plastic, and my ear looks like a cabbage patch doll...fix it!"

Tommy rubbed my arm in a desperate attempt to calm me down, but I elbowed his cancer ridden body away from me. He shrieked in pain, as he held his stomach and rushed over to a chair on the opposite side of the room.

"Now, Chloe, there's no need for the abusive language or physical violence. We're all adults here, who can communicate like adults," Dr. Kroon lectured.

"Fuck you and whatever the fuck you're talking about! Bastard, you can feel your face so don't tell me how to communicate. I paid a lot of money for this bull-shit ass plastic surgery," I added, then glanced over at Tommy. We both knew his rich-ass had paid for it, but my story sounded good.

"Well, I can understand your concern. But tell me, what are you feeling?" Dr. Kroon asked, with his pen and clipboard handy. He was obviously ready to take notes.

"What am I feeling? Didn't I just tell you that I couldn't feel anything?"

"Dear, the doctor is only trying to help," Tommy said uneasily in the background.

I turned around and stared at him, but to no avail. My face still wouldn't move, and everything was beginning to seem pointless.

"The numbness that you're experiencing may mean that a nerve has been pinched or injured. Swelling from the surgery might be putting pressure on the nerve as well." He paused and stared into my face. "Go ahead and wrinkle your forehead for me." I tried, but from the look on his face, it wasn't moving. "Your eyes seem to be tearing up also," he observed.

"How in the hell are you going to fix this, Doc?" I asked frantically.

"I want to keep you here for a while. I'm concerned that you may have some facial nerve paralysis, which is not unusual for someone who's had as much facial trauma as you have." He paused after seeing the anguish in my eyes. "It will heal though," he continued. "Trust me. You just have to stay two to three more weeks."

"Stay? I can't stay here. My family needs me," I cried, as I placed my fucked up face into the palms of my fucked up hands.

Tommy stood up and walked toward my bed. His movements were slow, and I could've sworn I heard bones cracking in the process. I stopped to wonder how he made his millions. He'd told me stories about being an investment banker and stockbroker. But most of it, I didn't believe. Especially the stories about the beautiful women he'd had. Tommy was hard on the eyes, but his pockets were loaded, so what the hell. Whatever he said, I would go along with.

"Doctor, thank you for your help, but can you please leave us alone for a second. I don't want her anymore upset than she already is."

Awwwww so sweet, I thought , clowning Tommy from my bed. He wanted to protect me...fucking sucka. I guess this was his way of letting me know that he had those capabilities.

"Certainly," Dr Kroon said, as he gathered up everything and left the room.

My plan was working just as I thought it would. I began crying harder and louder, as Tommy put his frail hand behind my neck, trying his best to console me.

"I just need to be with my family again. My daughter, she…she needs me. She's sick and she needs to be with her mother. Little girls shouldn't grow up without their mothers," I wailed, as the tears kept falling down my face.

"Your daughter? You never told me that you had a child," he said to me, sounding disappointed. "I told you that I had a thirty-two year old daughter who hasn't spoken to me in years. But you never told me anything about a daughter. Nothing," he added.

His voice carried a tone as if our bond had been broken by me not revealing my whole life to him, as he did to me. About his wife dying of cancer not too long before he was diagnosed with his. About his daughter, who couldn't wait for him to die so that she could get his inheritance. Something I secretly wished for. I planned on marrying his ass… becoming a rich bitch, getting money…the kind Anna Nicole Smith lucked up on.

"I'm sorry, Tommy. This is all way too much for me to bear. I don't have the money to pay for her hospital bills, or the money to get to where she is. I need to get to Rochester. I have to see my baby," I began screaming. "I just…maybe I'll just…kill myself!"

That was all I could think of before I grabbed my mirror and banged it against the steel post next to my bed, making it shatter everywhere. I grabbed a big piece of my seven years of bad luck and held it over my wrist to let Tommy know that I meant business.

"No, Chloe, don't!" was all I heard him say before I took the sharp glass and ran it across the veins on my wrist, opening up my skin and letting the dark blood trickle down my arm.

Staining my bed.

"Oh my God, somebody please help us!" Tommy shouted out, but not in enough time to stop the second slice to my skin.

My once untainted flesh now hung wide open as the heavy flow of blood continued to spill out. Realizing that no one had come to my aid, Tommy quickly grabbed some of my old, cloth bandages from off the edge of my bed, and tried his best to hold them tightly against my wounds. It was at this moment I wished I had AIDS.

So he would get infected and die.

But not before I could convince him to leave me his money.

Chapter Four
(Chloe)

"Damn. They really fucked you up!" Tuff said when I walked into his house.

It had been two weeks since I left out of the hospital without being discharged. Once I left on my own, I wasted no time flying into Rochester and catching a cab from the airport to Arnett Boulevard to go through with my plans. Even though my old man, Tommy, wanted me to listen to the doctor's warnings about me not being ready to leave the hospital yet, he still made sure I had as much money as I needed to make sure my "daughter" got the best health care that was available.

Tommy started me off with eight thousand dollars, which was all he could get his hands on at the moment and promised to deliver more soon, just as long as I didn't kill myself.

I agreed.

I did a little clothes shopping with the money before leaving Raleigh, and decided to save the rest just in case Tommy didn't come through with his promise, or died.

Men could never be depended upon.

That was just a set up for failure.

"What the hell are you talking about? My face is just a little swollen from the surgery, but I look fine," I said, trying to convince him and myself.

I walked over to the full length mirror he had leaning against his red living room wall, and noticed how much weight I had lost. *Damn, where did my ass go?* I asked myself, making a mental note to eat as much as I could to get my size back up. I was used to being thick in all the right places, and I was going to eat everything in sight to get back to the size eight I was used to. I refused to resemble anything like Oshyn's skinny-ass.

I'm glad it's still summer time, I thought, as I straightened out the Alice and Olivia t-shirt I wore, and pulled up my Rock and Republic jeans that seemed to be sagging. I'd gotten so used to North Carolina's weather that I was glad that winter hadn't come yet. My skin could no longer handle the blistering cold of Rochester's winter. The bandage that now covered my wrist in my necessary suicide attempt was still in place. I just stood there shaking my head at what a sad sight I was.

"Nah, you definitely fell off, Ma," he continued, snapping me out of my daze. "But I wasn't even talking about the surgery. I'm talking about how Oshyn and Brooklyn fucked you up."

He began to laugh.

My blood began to boil.

"No wonder you trying to find them. I would've made it my life's mission to get them back too if my face looked fucked up like yours!"

Tuff bent over and laughed so hard he didn't seem able to contain himself. I didn't see anything that funny, and couldn't believe that he would even play me like that. But he would pay.

"Like I said, faggot-ass nigga, my face is just a little swollen…that's all."

"Yeah, and like I said," he repeated as his laughter died down a bit, "you look crazy!"

30

As strong of a woman as I was, he kept poking at the one insecurity I had at the moment...my appearance. *Damn, my shit isn't that bad*, I thought to myself, and snuck one more glance at the mirror. My slanted brown eyes were still beautiful, and my skin, despite the war wounds, was still flawless.

My long, jet black hair was bone straight and settled near the bottom of my bra. Luckily, I had thick hair, keeping him from seeing the mutant ear I was desperately trying to hide. I stole myself away from the mirror after mentally building back up my self-esteem and turned my attention back toward him.

"Oh, okay. Well, you just wait until my baby, Brooklyn, finds out that his own cousin turned on him. We'll see who has the last laugh then."

At that very moment, it was me who was having the last laugh. Tuff was Brooklyn's first cousin, their mothers were sisters. The whole family hailed from Brooklyn, New York. Tuff was thirty-five and adjusting back into society after taking a ten year vacation in Attica. A bid he took for Brooklyn.

He'd only been out for a couple of months and decided to move to Rochester instead of going back home because he knew that this was where all the dudes came to get money. But he had a vendetta he wanted to settle. I guess while he was in jail, he heard about the high life that Brooklyn was living, and became salty when he was barely getting by with his commissary money.

But now that he was back out on the streets and had his money right again, this was his time to get Brooklyn back. He found out where I was through the streets and reached out to me, letting me know that we had the same goal in mind. The only difference was I was ready to kill. He wasn't.

Tuff was a shorter version of his cousin, standing only five eleven; definitely too short for my taste, but sorta stylish. They looked just alike though, with both carrying those deep dimples and dark skin. I was sure when they were younger, they were mistaken for brothers.

Wouldn't have surprised me if that were really the case.

Mothers weren't shit.

That was the one thing we had in common.

He wore black dreadlocks that barely grazed his shoulders and were neatly done. Kept himself up well though, just like my boo.

"What in the hell are you still laughing at?" he asked me, visibly upset that I had threatened to reveal to Brooklyn that he was my source.

"Who the fuck gave you the name Tuff anyway? They should've called you Bitch Ass Nigga instead. You're the worst."

I shook my head, disgusted that I had more balls than he did. Prison made him soft and afraid to go back, which tainted his ability to move like a real thug moved.

"I told Brooklyn that I was the only friend he had. I tried to warn him that I was the only person on this earth who wouldn't hurt him, but did he listen to me? Noooo! And now what is he left with? He's left with his own sorry-ass cousin turning him in for his own financial gain. That's not how you treat your family," I scolded.

"That nigga left me!" he yelled. "Ten years I did in Attica for him. Ten years for some drugs that weren't even mine!"

He felt the need to explain himself to me, which led me to believe that he felt a little guilty for his betrayal.

"I ought to shoot you in your face myself," was my threat to him. I was sure that Brooklyn still thought he had friends, but this was proof that money was still the only thing that made people cum. After all, a couple of hundreds was all it took for him to rattle off the phone number to me weeks ago.

"Word on the street was right," he said, as he picked a manila envelope off the couch and handed it to me. "Your

32

ass is crazy."

I tore the top of the envelope open before telling him, "Shut the fuck up," and pulled the contents out. I held in my hands three blank pieces of paper. "My patience is really starting to run thin with you, Tuff. What is this shit? Why are all these pages blank?" I asked, as I threw them in his face.

I was extremely calm. And if he knew anything about me, he'd be worried at my nonchalance.

"I was thinking…" He put his hand on his chin and rubbed it a little. "…If you would do anything to get them back for what they did to you, I'm sure that you wouldn't mind throwing in a couple extra thousand dollars. I have Brooklyn's whereabouts and other important information right here," he said, tapping on his back pocket.

He grinned, showing the same gap that lived in between Brooklyn's teeth. Showing the same love of money that I had. "Word on the street is that you have plenty of money and I want what you got," he said.

He turned his back to me as if I didn't matter. As if there was no way to negotiate his new terms. Yeah, I know I had close to seven thousand to move around with, but the reality of it all was that I was broke. I didn't have a dime to my name, and if it weren't for Tommy, and him falling in love with me at the hospital, I'd be in deep shit.

There was one thing I did have though that a man could never turn down; my sex appeal. With him being locked up for ten years, I knew that there was no way he could resist. I crept up behind him and slid my hands up his royal blue Christian Augier t-shirt. A blind person could tell that he spent a decade in jail just by the way his body was cut up and toned from all the heavy weight lifting people with nothing but time on their hands did.

I moved his hair out the way, closed my eyes and kissed the back of his neck, while he just stood there, refusing to make a sound. At this point, I wondered if I was the first woman's touch he'd felt since his release. The more I kissed him, the more he began to resemble his cousin.

I couldn't wait to be in his arms once again, so I closed my eyes and imagined that Tuff was Brooklyn. My nipples got hard and had begun poking through the white t-shirt I decided to take off, leaving me in my white lace Victoria's Secret bra.

This was what I had amounted to.

Cheap-ass Victoria's Secret.

I made my way in front of Tuff and took off the True Religion Jean Capri's I had on.

"Do you like what you see?" I whispered seductively, as I placed my arms around his broad chocolate neck.

The sweet smell of Sean John cologne hit my nose as I rubbed my pussy on him. Even though it looked like I had lost a few pounds, when my clothes came off you could tell that I still had curves, never losing my shape.

I closed my eyes and parted my lips slightly to finally feel what Brooklyn's lips now tasted like. I was only seconds away from making love to my man, but Tuff's dreads were getting in the way of my daydream. I held them back before I came to the realization that he wasn't the real thing, and I was abruptly pushed out of the way, which quickly snapped me into a harsh reality.

"Please, don't nobody give a damn about your worn out pussy," Tuff ranted. "anybody can get that shit!"

He stopped talking just for a moment to bend down and pick up my clothes off the floor, then forcefully shoved them into my arms.

"Worn out pussy?" I questioned, catching my clothes tightly in my arms. "Ten years you been letting them niggas bang your pussy out," I said, actually wondering how large his asshole had become.

He didn't allow what he really felt about my comments show. He stood tall, appearing to be unfazed as he picked in his teeth with a straw he pulled from his pocket.

"All I want is my fucking money. You know how this shit goes, baby. You aren't on top anymore. Bow down and pay your respect. It's a new king in town." He smiled again, thinking this shit was funny.

I looked Tuff up and down, with a frown on my face, letting him know that I was disgusted by the smallness of his new "king" status. Was the nigga asking for a blow job?

And then I laughed.

Hard.

"Me? Not on top? Yeah, you've been gone for way too long," I tried explaining to him, still snickering at this last comment. I was still very calm, which surely surprised him as much as it did me. Everyone was so used to me flipping off of emotions, that to see anything different was out of character for me. "But I can show you better than I can tell you who the boss still is."

"Is that supposed to be a damn threat?" Tuff asked, while squaring up on me. I guess his huge, flex-the-muscle scare tactic was something that worked while he was locked up, but it only caused more chuckles out of me.

"Nah, not a threat, baby. I don't make threats."

"You know what it is," he told me, muscles still flexed.

"Whateva, nigga."

He didn't scare me.

Rochester was my city.

The place where I was born and bred. And I'd be damned if I was going to let a bitch-ass Brooklyn nigga come in and mark his spot in my territory. I had more balls than he did, and today was the day that he'd die with them in his mouth.

My high of getting some dick was immediately replaced with the insatiable desire to get rid of him. Those were the only images I saw while I slipped my t-shirt and Capri's' back on. He turned his back on me and walked over to his pack of Newport cigarettes that lay open on the coffee table.

He put his guard down and underestimated me.

Bad mistake.

Huge.

I quietly picked up the small steel baseball bat that sat behind his couch. I'd caught a glimpse of it when I first walked in the house. While his fingers flickered with the lighter, attempting to light for his cigarette, I crept up behind him and cracked him over the head as hard as I could with the baseball bat.

In slow motion, the cigarette dropped to the floor.

He wasn't too far behind.

Tuff dropped to his knees, and when I made my way to his back pocket, I saw the blood trickling down his face. I dug inside, grabbing the piece of paper that sat neatly folded up and quickly unraveled it. *Jackpot*, I thought, as I read Brooklyn's address. The pain seemed to shock Tuff to a point where he wasn't moving and hadn't said a word. I guess it didn't take too long for him to see things my way.

Robbing him of any final words that a man scheduled to die was supposed to get, I banged the steel bat harshly against the front of his face. I listened to his skull crack open, and felt the warm blood splatter against my skin every time I swung. All thirty-six times.

The shit felt good.

So, I kept swinging.

Until I was sure he had crossed over to the other side.

However, at that point I still wasn't satisfied. Rage took over, so I stomped toward the kitchen.

This muthfucka better have a decent knife.

I wanted to make sure his ass was dead, so I vowed to stab him until he was cut into tiny pieces.

Chapter Five
(Oshyn)

"Where is he? You took my baby! Tell me where he is, or I swear to God I'll kill you!" Oshyn screamed.

I straddled him in the bed, trying my best to cut off his blood circulation with my legs as I held the butcher knife up to his neck. The tears streamed down my face as I desperately tried to find where Mye Storie had gone.

I saw the fear in Brooklyn's eyes as he lay on his back with his hands in the air. Since I climbed on top of him in his sleep, he had remained speechless, but found the nerve to somehow whisper, "Baby, please, don't do this. The kids are fine and..."

I put more pressure on his neck.

The knife was beginning to cut through.

"Stop it! Stop with all your fucking lies! You killed him! You killed the only son I had left!"

I had become hysterical, deranged almost, but for good reason. I was a mother who fought for her children because that was the only way they stayed safe. But I seemed to have failed again. Mye was gone and I was sleeping with the enemy. "I'll kill you if..."

Before I was able to finish my sentence, Brooklyn

37

snatched my head into his arms and yanked me into a head-lock while I was still on top of him. My long cream satin nightgown got in the way as I tried desperately to get back the knife that had fallen off the side of the bed.

He held me, and hugged me hard while I squirmed to break free. The beads of sweat that started popping out of his pores were now smeared on my face as he held me tighter; forcing me to inhale the Dove soap he'd used not too long ago to wash my sex off of his body. I found myself getting weaker and squirming a little less, as the tears mixed with snot trickled into my mouth.

"It's going to be okay," my husband promised me, as he gently laid my head on his shoulder and stroked my long hair back into its original place. "Everything is all going to be okay."

Lies.

Those were all lies.

I decided to take advantage of the situation while he still had my head buried in his armpits. My mouth opened wide, taking a big chuck of his meat into it, and biting down as hard as I could.

"Ahhhhhhhhhhh!" was all you heard. The sound echoed off the four walls of our room. Brooklyn forcefully pushed me off of him and onto the floor. "What the fuck is wrong with you, Oshyn? It's six o'clock in the morning and you're acting like a..."

His missing word was replaced with quick movement when he realized what I had back in my possession. He found himself on the other side of the bed just seconds before I swung at him. My thrust was fast, but it wasn't quick enough, because the end result was a puncture wound in our Vera Wang king sized mattress instead of his skin.

"Oshyn! Give me the fucking knife!"

Although he was on the other side of the bed, his hands were extended toward me, and his tone was that of a negotiator. He had obviously never perfected his negotiating skills, or he would have known that kind of tone would set me off. For his sake, he needed me to be as calm as possible. This was now a hostage situation that Brooklyn thought he was going to be able to talk me out of.

But he was wrong.

Dead wrong.

"You…took…my…baby!"

The steady flow of warm tears that streamed down my face mimicked the falls at Niagara Falls. All I wanted were answers, and he wasn't giving them to me. I started walking around the bed, trying to get closer to him, and he in turn, started walking in the other direction.

"Stop and think about what you're doing right now." He squirmed a little, as he touched the huge bite mark I'd left on him. "Bella and Mye are still asleep. I didn't kill anybody. Just put the knife down. I'll take you to where they are."

I felt myself hyperventilating, so I put my head down for a moment to catch my breath. Before I could look back up, Brooklyn had leaped across the bed and had thrown me to the ground, taking the knife right out of my hand.

Unable to pry myself up from the cold, chocolate hardwood floors, I just laid there, wondering when all this pain was going to end. I looked up and noticed that Brooklyn was gone. I wasn't sure where he went, but when he came back there was nothing in his hand that I could hurt anyone with. He scooped me up off the floor into his strong arms and laid me back on the bed.

Like I was originally.

Before all of this began.

When he laid his body on top of mine, I was surprised as to how weightless his body felt. "Get off of me!" I demanded.

I really didn't mean those words, which were proven by my actions of not putting up a fight. I was slowly snapping out of whatever state of mind I had put myself in. He said nothing back. Just covered me like a blanket, trying to force me to go back to sleep.

Like I was a baby who needed to be pacified.

"Oshyn," he said. I ignored him, but he wouldn't give up. "You've been through things that no human being should ever have to experience, and you've done it with no one to really talk to and help you through these times." He paused, waited for me to respond, and when I didn't he continued. "Baby, you know that you always have me to talk to, but I don't think that I can bring you through the demons you're dealing with. You're going to have to go to counseling."

I shifted my body from side to side while he still towered on top of me, uneasy about the words that were coming out of his mouth.

"I'm fine now," I assured him. "I'm sure I was just having a bad dream, but everything is alright now. I don't need counseling."

He shook his head, but not before blurting out, "No, you're not okay. I'm pretty sure that mental health is on my insurance. But even if it isn't, I'll pay the expenses no matter how much it costs, for however long you need it. I'll do whatever it takes to get back the Oshyn I fell in love with."

"So, you're not in love with me?" I asked, confused about his last remark. "Am I not the same Oshyn?"

"Of course I'm still in love with you, but something is wrong, and we have to figure it out. The kids need you. I need you. So, like I said, money is of no object…whatever it takes."

Brooklyn made great money at the hotel, enough money to pay all the bills himself, while allowing me to be a full time mother. Rooms at that expensive, five star hotel had to be booked months in advance, and it was a place where all the clients had black cards. They even had ports where helicopters brought their guests to private parties in villas. A town where their main way of getting money was tourism. A town where everyone who worked in the hotel industry was able to afford a more than decent lifestyle for their families.

I snapped out of my thoughts and found myself bursting into tears. Depression seemed to be hitting me hard, and it wasn't a burden I felt I could tackle by myself.

"Shhh, it's going to be okay," Brooklyn promised.

"I just miss Chloe so much," I revealed. "You tried though. You tried your best to get rid of her and she didn't deserve any of it!"

Even in my deranged state, I watched once again as sadness filled my husband's eyes, along with his curiosity about my health and sanity. I placed my hands on his chest and pushed him off of me, quickly getting myself off the bed before he could put me back on it.

"What are you doing?" he wondered, as he watched me go into my closet and throw all of my clothes on the floor.

"I'm packing my bags. Going back to the states. Need to find Chloe and talk to her." I was frantically running around, trying to put something together and into a suitcase.

"But she's dead, babe. She's gone forever."

"No. She never died. You didn't kill her."

He put his head down like a puppy who had just chewed up a new pair of Christian Louboutin stilettos and knew that he was in for an ass whooping. I knew that this was the best time to get some kind of truth out of him.

"Tell me the truth, Brooklyn! I already know it. I just want you to say it out loud, that it was Chloe that was calling here the other day!"

Silence.

He never lifted his head back up.

"Please stop making me out to be crazy. For the sake of my sanity, tell me the truth!" I said, trying to drill the guilt in his head. "Tell me who was on the other end of the phone that night."

He slowly brought his head back up, barely making eye contact, and parted his lips enough to say, "You're right. It *was* Chloe on the phone. She's still alive."

Chapter Six
(Chloe)

Finally.

Living good again.

I lay stretched out in my lounger, feeling the effects of my third Mojito, as I watched my sweet and savory man, Brooklyn, make drinks from behind the bar. He looked good. Damn good. I guess the time spent away from him made me forget how sexy he really looked in his clothes. His bulging arms, tight waist, and firm abs made me squirm all across the cushion. Maybe it was the all white he wore, which made his muscles appear larger and sexier than before.

Then again maybe it wasn't the color of his clothes. My skinny waiter had on white too, yet was so thin that he looked like he'd just finished smoking a pound of crack. He'd been by my private section a few times, asking if I wanted another drink. Kept bragging on the bartender, talking about how good he was, and how even the locals crowded his bar every day for his famous creations. I wanted to tell Rosario, or whatever the fuck his crazy-ass name was, that I was well aware of how good the bartender was. I wanted to tell him that I knew Brooklyn very well, and would be fucking him in front of his dead wife by the end of the night.

Instead, I tilted my tan oversized, floppy hat, and lifted

43

my cup of ice as soon as I saw him headed my way. That should've given him the clue that I was good for the moment. I needed peace…just time to monitor Brooklyn's every move. The spot I chose proved to be perfect. I sat about seven yards away underneath a large umbrella and a five foot three petition in front of me. It was a fake-me-out private cabana, but worked well. I knew it would be difficult for him to see me laid back on the plush lounge chair draped in my incognito gear. Especially since his bar was packed…and he, crazy busy, making one drink after another for the loud bar hoppers. Luckily, the pool was behind me, and kept the extra noise away.

It was nearly ninety-eight degrees, so my body adhered to the weather. My sexy two-piece held together by two skinny strings would've driven any man to their knees, especially if I decided to take off the matching sarong that straddled my thighs. I remained still, showing off the tanned skin of my bare, oily legs. It was all I would show for the moment. I didn't want to attract any unnecessary attention. My purpose was to watch Brooklyn like a hawk through my retro, oversized sunglasses until he got ready to leave work and head home.

While watching him, my glamour thing had obviously attracted a little bit of attention. From the expensive Dolce and Gabanna shades, to my freshly polished toes, to the four hundred dollar Bottega Venetta pumps, to my freshly waxed pussy, made me a target. Although I stayed far away from the action around the bar, it seemed as if I had attracted some unwanted attention from one of the vendors opposite the bar.

Maybe it was the way my boobs sat nipple first greeting everyone. It was puzzling, almost scary. I wasn't sure why this deep, dark-skinned woman with a crib-sized sheet wrapped around her head eyed me from afar. When my eyes got a chance to examine her small white tent and the contents, I became curious. The sign read - See Your Future. I thought, *bullshit*. I'd rather spend my money with the jewelry guy, or the lady with the hand painted mask. At least I could scare the shit out of Oshyn.

It seemed every chance the woman got she would wave me over with her hand. I just closed my eyes because her sales pitch was whack. The glare spelled evil...didn't crack a smile, and never even made a move. She just sat staring, waiting for me to open my eyes again. I thought about moving, but was distracted by Brooklyn taking off his linen shirt. He'd apparently spilled something red on his shirt and was now in a tight, white wife beater.

Damn, I shouted inside, then raised my hand to block the strong rays from the sun.

The ugly bitch still stared, but needed to be blocked from my mind. *It was all about Brooklyn*, I told myself, slipping my hands into my bikini bottom. I closed my eyes, ready to dream. To feign. Ready to get my thing off. I thought about me and Brooklyn on the beach.

Alone.

Words couldn't express how horny I got when I got the vision of his body on top of mine. It was me and him grinding right on the lounger, right on the beach. "Oh hell yeah," I whispered to myself.

The more my body moved, the hornier I became. Even with my eyes closed tightly, the scene seemed so surreal. My fingers massaged my smooth bald pussy briskly, while my mouth fought hard not to shout out. Lately, I'd become Queen of masturbation, and had the world record on cumming from a finger. But Brooklyn always brought out the best in me.

I thought about the ice in my cup and opened my eyes to grab a few cubes. Something new, something different always sparked my interest. I was still in the zone, but wanted to take it a step further. My vagina throbbed for a dick, a hard one...but fingers and ice would have to do. I was already wet, but needed to get soaked. I moved a little more, squirming in the seat, and allowing each cube to press against my clit.

45

The coldness excited me. Had me going wild. I didn't give a fuck who saw me or my weird facial expressions. I kept grinding, and swaying my hips from side to side, while melting pieces of ice with my hot pussy. The shit felt so damn good I was willing to cum with or without Brooklyn. Just when I was about to cum, I got creative and inserted a piece of ice into my pussy, pretending it was the best dick I'd ever had. Of course it melted. Then I took a deep breath as I nutted inside of my bathing suit and all over the seat. The shit was so good. I reached for another piece of ice, but was interrupted by the ringing of my cell phone. It said *Unknown*. I hated that shit, and hated that somebody was trying to sabotage my sex life.

"What!" I shouted into the phone.

"Chloe, what's wrong? I was calling to check on you." Tommy's voice sounded concerned, and even though I knew he meant well, I just wasn't the compassionate type.

"How can I help you?" I snapped.

"You okay? I haven't heard from you since you left the hospital."

"I didn't want to get you involved. This is too much for you to handle," I told him with sorrow. "My baby...my baby... my baby," I kept repeating. "I'm not sure how things are gonna turn out."

"Chloe, listen to me...," Tommy began.

"No, you listen to me!" I flipped out, sat straight up, and decided playing games wasn't on the agenda for the day. "I need ten thousand and fast!" I shouted. "I'll explain later, but if you plan on being with me, send it through Western Union. Today!" I barked.

"But...but....but...Chloe..."

"No buts... you old fucker! If you wanna run with a bad bitch, get that money sent. If not, stay on the porch and I'll see you when I see you."

There was silence.

Then breathing.

Maybe he'd had a heart attack and left me his money

anyway. Then that thought was quickly ruined. "Ten thou-sand," he confirmed in a meek tone.

"Exactly." My tone showed no remorse. And he knew I meant business. "I'll be back at home in a few days," I added, using my sweet voice. "I got something for you, Daddy," I sang, then hung up and turned to my left.

There she was again. Sitting. Staring. Every time we made eye contact, it became more obvious she was watch-ing me just as much as I was watching her.

"Come, let me share your future!" she shouted in her light, foreign accent.

I hopped up angrily, pulled my sarong tighter and waltzed over toward the tent. As I got closer, a bizarre feel-ing came over me. Almost warning me not to buck at the woman and not to sit down. I looked back over my shoulder at Brooklyn, only to see him shaking a container back and forth, and grinning from ear to ear at the slut leaning toward his frame.

"You like," the old woman spoke in a ghostly tone. "Sit down," she told me.

Instantly, an eerie feeling came over me. I quickly scanned the two tables underneath the tent, noticing small clear jars labeled healing potions, unlit candles, and strong odorous powders scattered about. Even speckles of tiny red particles, which reminded me of crushed red peppers, cov-ered the small table topped with an old, laced white table-cloth.

"Sit sassy girl, and look into my eyes."

She was an old woman...my guess in her late seven-ties, with tons of lines running across her face. I had never let another bitch scare me....ever...but she was working on making me a punk. First, my eyes darted toward one of her signs. Wise One...it read. I looked at her.

She looked back at me.

Hesitantly, I sat in the only white wobbly chair avail-able. It was lop-sided, and felt like she'd owned it for years. As soon as I sat down, the bitch pulled out a jar of more of that red shit and swiftly started sprinkling it on me.

I flipped. "What the fuck, old lady!"

"It's love powder, my dear." She blew it on me. "Believe me, it will bring you love, money and power," she said slowly.

Of course I calmed down. "Any man I want?" I asked, with a smirk that spread about my face.

"Any man," she confirmed.

"How much is this shit?" I asked, while going into my bra.

She paused, which gave me a chance to get a good look at her frail skin. Her arms lacked moisture…my assumption from working in the sun daily. And the pit of her eyes, sunken in, allowing her bubbly eyeballs to bulge even more. A piece of her wool-like hair peeked from her wild-looking scarf. And the long, African dress, which fell well below her ankles, didn't add much to her style either.

"Ten for the basics," she finally said. "Twenty for the good stuff, and thirty if you want to know how to control your men."

"This shit is a scam. I knew I shouldn't have come over here!"

"You think?" she challenged me with her voice. "I have the power to bring good or bad."

"Ohh…"

All of a sudden she grabbed my hand tightly, as if the intent was to ruff me up for my money. I simply closed my fist and gave her the look of death. "I'll give you twenty," I told her.

"Your life," she said, gazing into my eyes and squeezing my hand tighter. "Your palm tells me there are two men."

My eyes lit up. Then once again, I checked on Brooklyn. "Take the thirty," I told her.

She released her grip, took the money, and sat it off to the side with the other money in her small metal box. My first thought- *this lady's making a killing*. The stack seemed to be roughly three to four hundred bills. I tried to count further, but was interrupted by the tightness of the grip she'd taken on both my hands.

"Two men. Both good looking. Both in love with you," she ranted. "One man you know. The other you will soon meet."

Her words made my heart thump.

"Amazing sex. And money," she mumbled to herself.

Now, she was talking some shit that I wanted to hear.

"Amazing sex?" I questioned with a smile.

"Yes, who's this guy I see with you? He's tall, a dark man." She said a few other words, but in a much stronger accent, so I couldn't comprehend. But I'd heard enough. I was sold.

"Oh shit, you are real!" I shouted. *The bitch is describing Brooklyn*, I told myself shockingly. "Tell me more. Are we married! A baby! What? Tell me!"

"Oh…noooooo…nooooo," she uttered, with a disappointing shake of her head. "He's with another lady now. But there is someone else for you. He has money too."

"That's what I want to hear. Positive shit. Nothing negative," I instructed.

"Money is good. But things won't go so good for you. You need some of my powder," she added, while sprinkling some more of that bullshit on me before I could dodge it.

"That's enough," I warned.

"No, really. Somebody will pay you back," she continued in a chilling tone. "You've done something really bad, but your payback will be greater. Death, I see death," she repeated.

I tried to pry her hand off of mine. "I said that's it! Now shut the fuck up, old lady!"

"My mouth may close, but it doesn't change your fate. Ill-fated love affair," she chanted. "Ill-fated love affair."

Without hesitation, I kicked at her feet with force. At the same time, my eyes darted from right to left to see who watched us nearby, or from afar. It was at that moment that I saw him leaving. It was my man in a hurry leaving work like

49

something was wrong. Like he'd seen a ghost or some shit.

Immediately, I kicked the woman even harder. It didn't take long for her to loosen her grip and for me to snatch her small box holding the money. As soon as I had the loot, *her money*, successfully in hand we locked eyes. I was already on my feet and moving, but still couldn't dodge the horrible smelling dust she blew my way.

"A hex is what you've caused me to do," she said angrily. "My revenge will come at the hands of someone else, but you will die and burn in hell," she warned.

"Oh yeah, well I'll meet you there," I countered as I fled the scene.

I wanted to shout back some more, letting her know I didn't believe in hexes, roots, or any of that shit, but decided against it. With the old woman's money in hand, I jetted toward the parking lot, hoping I hadn't left anything behind. My money was in my bra, and my purse was in the car I'd rented, so whatever Rosario could steal and sell was all his. I had to catch Brooklyn racing from the lot in the Range Rover he drove away in.

By the time I'd hopped in the rental car, Brooklyn was out of sight. I was still huffing and puffing, trying to catch my breath, as I turned the steering wheel frantically. Car after car, I dodged, swerved in and out of traffic, searching for a glimpse of his truck.

The full chase was on his black ass, yet it wasn't enough. Then my breakthrough came. I saw the back of his truck about ten cars ahead of me turning by a large bend. I sped up, then forced a few cars into the dirt on the side of the road. *He's not gonna outsmart me*, I told myself, wiping off particles of bullshit the voodoo bitch had sprinkled on me.

Then I heard it.

A fender bender ahead.

Some bitch hit three old ladies in a station wagon, causing a six car back-up and causing my man to disappear...again.

Chapter Seven

(Oshyn)

I waited outside, pacing our narrow driveway, while I looked for any sign of Brooklyn pulling up. Mye got increasingly heavier as I pulled him up on my hip. It was late in the evening, and the temperature was still a scorching ninety-eight degrees, with no signs of letting up.

"Mye, let go!" I demanded, as he eagerly managed to grab a chunk of my hair, tangling a few strands into his chubby little hands. Drool began to drip down to the rolls of his shirtless stomach, while he laughed at my frustration.

"Bella, come and get your brother!" I yelled.

No answer.

I gave her the benefit of doubt because I was all the way outside and she may not have heard me. But I sort of knew that wasn't the case.

"Bella!"

"What?" she sassed, making her presence known at the front door. She stepped outside in her pink Juicy Couture sundress, which gave her the deceiving look of an angel, even though she was anything but.

"What?" I repeated softly, yet angry deep inside.

I thought that her talking back situation had been cleared up six months ago, and couldn't quite figure out why it was resurfacing as a problem now. I hated to think it, but maybe Brooklyn had a good point about us going to counseling. Judging from Bella's attitude, and where I assumed it was headed, it wouldn't hurt. It had begun to rain, and although Mye was enjoying the raindrops, I wanted to keep him dry.

"Here, I need you to take Mye with you inside the house. Play with him some…just keep him out of this rain and out of my hair for a while."

I extended my baby to her, making the choice to ignore the argument that we would have if I mentioned how she spoke to me. At this point in my life, I had bigger issues to deal with, and I wanted to choose my battles wisely.

It had been about a half an hour since Brooklyn called in a panic. He said he was leaving work and rushing home…had some news to tell me. I knew I couldn't take much more. The voices were back, and this time I didn't want to hear them alone. My grandma, my mother, Apples and Micah had all returned to me once again, trying to warn me about something that left me tossing and turning during my nap.

Their presence that once filled me up with comfort and warmth today left me frightened and alone. I had to admit, I hadn't been myself lately, but I knew this time I needed help before I snapped.

"Whatever," was what Bella blurted out after taking my son. She rolled her little green eyes and turned to go back inside the house. "I'm tired of watching him. You're the mom…that's your job!"

I tried hard to ignore her, but this time it wasn't happening. I snapped.

"Come back here!" I shouted like Joan Crawford from the movie, *Mommy Dearest*. My face was balled up into a serious knot, and my fists were balled tightly down by my sides. "You hear me!" I warned again.

As soon as Bella was within a few feet of me, I grabbed Mye out of her arms, dropped him on the wet grass, which cushioned his fall and reached for the back of her rain soaked sundress. After noticing her trying to get away, I yanked her scrawny-ass backwards, and punched her in her side with all the strength my fist could muster up. I hit her like she was a grown woman because that's what she acted like. Miss Bella needed to be taught a lesson.

"Owwww!" was the constant noise that escaped out of her mouth, which now matched Mye's screams.

He managed, in all his confusion, to crawl to me, only to have me shoo him away like a fly. His cries only got louder as I locked my fingers into her light brown spiraled hair, and pulled with every intention of making her bald.

"Pleaseeeee…I'm sorry," Bella confessed, as her fair skin turned into the color of a delicious red apple. Her little hands did what they could to pry mine off of her, but with every attempt she made, I yanked harder.

"Please…let…go!"

That was the last thing I heard before I wrapped my other hand around her throat. Before her little lungs began gasping for air. Before she struggled to inhale the air that freely floated past her. Before she could no longer breathe. At the same time that I was on a mission to kill, a crack of thunder sounded in the air, and a heavy downpour of rain gushed from the sky without warning.

While I choked Bella like a stranger on the streets, my ears flipped outward when the sound of screeching tires were heard. Seconds later, Brooklyn pulled up in the Range Rover like a madman. Without hesitation, he jumped from the car, and tried to pry me off of Bella. His strength was un-beatable, but I sure as hell tried. Before I knew it, Brooklyn had overpowered me and set Bella free. Soaking wet, I panted, sweated, and resembled a crazy woman detained in the wet grass, sitting with my hands behind my back.

Mye stopped his wailing only after being rescued by his daddy, and watched on as Bella coughed violently. While she attempted to get her regular breathing pattern back, I sat defiantly in the soaking wet grass. We all behaved like a bad storm wasn't really brewing. Well, then again, none of us were normal for the moment. I couldn't believe that I had snapped like that, but hopefully she had learned her lesson. Otherwise, it was clear that I would do it again, with no one to stop me.

While Brooklyn rushed the kids inside to get dry, I remained outside, pacing our tiny front yard, trying to make sense of what was happening with me.

My mind was an empty canvas.

With remnants of going senile.

I stood in place, emotionless, watching the rain alternate between mild to gushes of water. If I didn't know any better, I'd say that things couldn't get any worse than this, but I knew better and that thought was just too good to be true.

About ten minutes went by before Brooklyn emerged from the house. He stood in front of me, scratching his head and uttering the words, "I don't know." He looked down at the ground and continued scratching an itch I knew didn't exist. I watched him, trying my best to decipher what his statement meant.

All of my frustrations got so heavy that my tears started pouring out without giving me a chance to prepare for them. His scratching had finally come to an end and he stepped forward, grabbing me in his arms where I felt safe.

"I don't know," he whispered once again, pulling me tighter into his embrace. "I got news that my cousin, Tuff, died," he informed me slowly. "Killed... stabbed over forty times. Found dead in his home. He was there for like two days," he said, getting choked up. "And then I come home to this."

His shocking news stopped me in my tracks, and I suddenly felt bad about not being able to control my situation. I realized how much stress I'd been putting on him.

"I'm so sorry, baby."

I unconsciously wiped my nose on his wet linen work shirt, leaving it with the remains of my sadness. The rain seemed to slow up a bit, which made me ask if he wanted to go inside.

He ignored my comment.

"He was only thirty-five, the only cousin I had," Brooklyn said, with a strained voice.

We stood in the front yard hugging like two lovers in the rainstorm who needed one another, until Brooklyn got silent, as if he were daydreaming about his cousin. His eyes were glossy, and he looked into the cloudy sky, just staring, thinking, hurting. I wanted to help him but didn't know what to say.

Tuff was his first cousin, and although he was just a few years older than Brooklyn, he treated him like he was his father, before getting locked up and having to do a ten year bid. I wasn't sure if they had talked much since his release a few months ago, but I knew that he was someone Brooklyn held dear to his heart.

"She has a phone call," Bella said, peeking her head out the door.

She deliberately ignored me and addressed Brooklyn only.

"Take a message," Brooklyn told her, unable to handle any more drama for the day. "I have to go to Rochester to help with the funeral arrangements," he then said to me.

I kept thinking about Tuff. "You never told me that Tuff lived in Rochester." I had a puzzled look on my face. "I don't understand what would make him go to Rochester after spending all that time upstate."

"Yeah. He didn't want to go back to Brooklyn. He said it was too much trouble there. But anyways, I'm going to need for you and the kids to come with me. After walking into the mess I just saw, I can't leave you here alone with them."

My jaw hung low.

He talked to me like his trust had taken its toll. Why would he offend me like that? Like I was a mother who would harm her children?

"Let's hurry," he ordered, confirming that I was leaving

55

St. Tropez with him.

      I guess I didn't have much of a choice.

Chapter Eight
(Chloe)

The rain came down.

Torrentially.

The kind of downpour that made you look like you had been swimming all day, even if in it for a few seconds. The hail of water that fell from the sky seemed to come from nowhere, as it was only just fifteen minutes prior that I was chilling in sunny conditions. And as I vividly remembered the forecast, it was supposed to remain sunny and clear all day.

Fucking liars, I accused the weatherman, as I struggled to keep up with Brooklyn. I had already lost him once, but managed to catch back up with him after driving on two wheels, and on the wrong side of the road. I desperately hoped that he was leading me to where he lived. They lived. The bitch Oshyn lived.

Tuff had gotten over on me when I initially got the address from him. It was the address to Brooklyn's job, and not their home. I made a mental note to have somebody spit on the nigga at his funeral. Although I had reservations about how everything would go down, ten minutes later Brooklyn pulled into the driveway of a big beautiful house.

"Jackpot," I said to myself. They were living large. Just

as Oshyn had always done, and as much as I hated to admit it, their house was surprisingly gorgeous.

The sight of Brooklyn fanatically running from his truck snapped me back into reality as I realized what was going on.

Bella's feet were off the ground.

Oshyn's hands around her neck.

I chuckled as I watched the man of the house stop a cat fight between a child and a grown-ass woman. *Just like Oshyn,* I thought to myself*, always trying to scare somebody smaller than her.* I recalled the day in the bookstore when a chick spit in her face and she didn't do anything. Fuckin' sucka!

I looked on as Brooklyn grabbed his son off the ground and led Bella, who was gasping for air, into the house. Even though I should've killed the little bitch when I had the chance, she was turning into a beautiful girl. Reminded me of me when I was that age. *Maybe it's not too late to put her on the payroll*, I contemplated, always thinking of a way to come up.

With Brooklyn making sure the kids were safe in the house, Oshyn was left by herself outside. Where it was just me, her, and nothing but time. The rain continued to fall harder, soaking Oshyn, and causing her clothes to cling to her body. The wipers barely gave me just enough visibility to notice that she had gained some weight. She wasn't fat, but thick.

Just how Brooklyn liked it.

Just how Brooklyn liked it on me.

Her hair was drenched, but I saw that it was longer than mine was, and even though she seemed to be stressed about something, she still looked like money. I fought the urge to hop out of the car and handle her once and for all, because I needed to remember that my time would come. I needed to make sure that it would be perfect.

Not deterred by the storm, Brooklyn came back out of the house and they began to talk. Since my car wasn't a familiar one in the neighborhood I felt like a parked car with the windshield wipers on were drawing unwanted attention, so I quickly turned them off. And was left with foggy, steamy windows.

I couldn't see them.

They couldn't see me.

Reminded me of the days I use to enjoy having sex in the car. While it rained as hard as it was raining today, I turned on the air condition and waited as it defrosted the windows. It seemed pointless to sit outside blindly stalking, but it would be all worth it at the end of the day. I honestly couldn't believe that I was able to get this close to her so soon. I thought that it was going to take some time, even years before I got a chance to go through with my revenge. But here it was a short six months later and I was in front of her house.

This time she would die.

Oshyn and her whole family.

I contemplated leaving their son, Mye, out of this, but he had both of their blood running through his veins. A line I had to cut because I couldn't risk him carrying on their name. Harmless now would turn into dangerous later, and I couldn't let that happen. At almost two years old, he was just a casualty of war; like his big brother, Micah, had been. My intentions for Bella was to bury her alive. To know that she would be six feet under suffocating from dirt warmed my heart.

And Brooklyn, my sweet Brooklyn, would get one more chance. He would be with me or he would be with no one. The choice was his. If he chose to stay with me, we would live happily ever after like I dreamed. We would go back to the way things were when he would come home and make love to me.

When *we* were in love.

Before Oshyn found out and ruined it all.

But if he chose to stay with her, death would do them part into a million little pieces, literally. I would chop their bodies up and spread the pieces all over whatever city I decided to kill them in.

I continued to daydream and contemplate how I was going to flawlessly execute my plan, and get away with their demise. The last of my family. After them, there was no more heritage until I reproduced.

The heavy rain continued to hit the car, and without thinking twice, my thoughts shifted to the old lady who read my palms. I still had no idea where her spooky-ass had come from, and even though I didn't believe in that shit, a part of me wished that the thought of me actually being in love wasn't too good to be true.

I closed my eyes and envisioned my mystery man being tall, dark and handsome; like Brooklyn, but better. I couldn't wait to get Oshyn out of the way so that I could finally get on with my life and start a family of my own.

A crack of thunder blasted through the sky, frightening me and snapping me from my thoughts. I glanced at the time on my dashboard and realized that a little over an hour had gone by since I first parked my car in front of the house and that everyone had gone inside. There wasn't any movement in the house so I got antsy. It wasn't just their house that seemed motionless, but the whole neighborhood looked desolate.

Erie.

As if they knew that something was getting ready to pop off. If they knew what I knew, they were better off inside because my wrath was bigger and stronger than the rainstorm. I decided to pick up my International Blackberry and call the house.

It rang.

Twice.

"Hello?" Oshyn said.

Oshyn's voice still sounded the same as I listened to her tell Brooklyn that, "she's still calling." It was beyond me why they hadn't changed the phone number yet, but she had never been too swift when it came to common sense shit. I hung up the phone and sat back for several minutes to relax

60

a little. My patience was beginning to run thin when I noticed something through my car window. The rain storm refused to clear up and I struggled to see past the glass that I looked through.

  With strained eyes, I looked on as Brooklyn and Oshyn rushed out of the house to put a few big suitcases in their truck. *What in the hell is going on here?* I wondered, as I watched Bella run out of the house and quickly threw her pink suitcase in with the rest of the bags. They all seemed to be incredibly unfazed by the massive rainstorm, which by now had them all completely drenched. Oshyn and Bella jumped in the car, and I watched Brooklyn as he ran back into the house and back out with their son.

  The son that he was supposed to have with me.

  The son she killed.

  The son that I would return the favor to.

  While he locked the front door to the house, I couldn't help but to wonder if they knew I was in the rental car stalking them. Did the frequent phone calls to the house give me away? *Why else would they be leaving in such a hurry?* I asked myself, wondering if Tuff had tipped them off. It was like I had always said before…no one was to be trusted.

  No one seemed to notice the presence of my car parked in front of their house as they backed out of their driveway and drove right past me. Refusing to be left behind, I cranked up my car and followed right behind them, being careful not to tail too closely. My windshield wipers squeaked as the rain became more intense again. Although I could barely see anything that was in front of me, the storm turned out to be a great camouflage.

  I followed them up and down the rough and narrow alleys that their country called streets, and had a less than smooth drive on the bumpy cobblestone paved roads.

BEEP! BEEP! BBEEEEPPP!

  The horn of the Range Rover sounded as a woman with two young kids crossed the street without a care. Brooklyn dodged the catastrophe and slammed on breaks, while I

61

pressed on the gas, hoping to teach her a lesson. I rolled down my window and stuck out my head, as the twenty-something year old looked back like she'd done nothing wrong.

"You stupid bitch!" I screamed, as she and her children made it safely to the sidewalk. Realizing she'd dropped something, she darted back out into the street, causing me to come to a screeching halt, while the Range Rover drove away. Wanting to jump out of my car and whip her ass, I decided that it would be best to continue on with my mission.

The next bitch who runs in front of this car is going to get run the fuck over! I thought to myself, as I pressed my foot on the gas, hoping to catch back up with them. Relieved that they hadn't gotten too far, and with only one car in between us, I had caught back up. Impatience was building up, as thoughts of running them off a cliff crept in my mind, yet I managed to stay focused. I followed them for an additional half an hour, before noticing the sign of our final destination.

Nice Cote D'Azure Airport.

Where in the fuck are y'all going? I asked myself, as they looked around for a parking space. Oblivious to the other cars that were all around me, I accidentally banged my rental into a parked Bentley.

Hard.

And it was then that we locked eyes.

Me and Oshyn.

She paused.

Never blinked.

Never got anyone else's attention to verify that it was me. She just stared at me with a look of delusion as I hopped out the rental, leaving it behind for someone else to deal with. I got it under an alias anyway and could've cared less what the consequences were. I had bigger problems.

My cover had been blown.

Chapter Nine

(Chloe)

"I need a ticket out of here right now!" I demanded like a lunatic.

In my outside voice.

The chick that was behind the counter at International Air looked at me like I was crazy. I'd caused an uproar, a scene I'm sure that she wasn't use to. She probably hadn't seen a bitch like me other than in the movies.

This was Saint Tropez.

Not the hood.

"I mean, do you speak fucking English?" I asked her, as I slammed my fist on the counter that stood between us. She didn't have too long to answer, or her head would be slammed against the hard surface. I turned my head viciously from side to side, mimicking the exorcist, as I tried finding someone else capable of taking care of my request.

"What the fuck are y'all muthafuckas looking at?" I screamed into the crowd of white tourists, who were just waiting to get home from a relaxing weekend. No one dared to answer.

Oshyn, Brooklyn and the children had already gone through security, and I wasn't sure where they were going or what flight that were taking, but if I had to take a guess, it was Rochester. Tuff's funeral was in a few days, and Brooklyn wouldn't have missed that.

"Hello, Miss, can I help you with something?" a chunky man with a receding hairline asked. He snapped me from my daze. "What seems to be the problem?"

"What seems to be the problem?" I asked rhetorically, as I looked at his tag that read *Manager*, and was relieved that I was finally able to get the situation resolved. "The problem is that I need an emergency flight back to Rochester, New York right now! There was a death in the family, and my sister is on the plane as we speak. We need to travel together!"

"I see," he said in his French accent, while typing a few things into his computer.

With two fingers.

Moving as slow as a fucking turtle.

"Are you serious? Dude, can you *not* move any faster than that?"

"Ma'am, I'm…"

"Ma'am? Do I fucking look like a Ma'am to you? I'm twenty-eight years old. And if you don't hurry your fat-ass up, you're going to have a serious problem on your hands!" I warned.

"I'm moving as fast as I can!" he replied with an attitude, never looking up to make eye contact. He typed a few more things then stopped, before slowly lifting his head and looking at me. "I'm sorry but that last flight to Rochester is sold out." He typed a little more. "The next flight I have doesn't leave until tomorrow afternoon. Would you like me to book that one for you?"

"If you don't get me out of here right now, I'm going to kill you!"

Acting like a four year old kid having a temper tantrum, I knocked all the brochures and advertisements off the counter, and was ready to go to war when someone caught my eye.

64

He stood six foot four, with skin the color of black maple. I peeped that his clothes were custom-made, and the snakeskin briefcase topped off my assumption.

He had plenty money.

Maybe he was who the old woman saw in my future?

Brushing off the idea, I diverted my attention back to the manager, and was met by four security officers instead of a plane ticket.

"Ma'am, can you please come with us?" the one guy said, with an even thicker French accent than the manager. He was the shortest one, standing five foot two, while all the taller men loomed over me.

"Fuck you, you little midget! And *hell no*, I can't go with you anywhere. He's *going* to get me a flight and I'm *going* to get on that plane with my family, and you all are *going* to leave me the fuck alone!"

Steam rose from my head, as I watched a crowd form around me and point their fingers in my direction. One of the bigger security officers grabbed my arm and yanked me up like I was a rag doll.

"You don't have a choice," he roared, as he dragged me away from the counter. I swung at his face with the one hand that I had free and caught his jaw. He wrapped his huge bicep around my neck and put me in a headlock, dragging me away.

"I'm going to blow this bitch up!" I threatened, while gasping for air. "I'm coming back and I'm going to kill all of you!"

I ended up all alone in what looked like an interrogation room, and for a moment I regretted not handling everything a little smoother. With all the commotion I attracted to myself, I was sure all chances of me catching up with Oshyn had been ruined. It would now take a miracle to change this situation around, yet I was still going to try to work my magic.

As I contemplated how I was going to get myself out of this mess, the steel door opened up, and a strong muscleman that looked like a French version of Mike Tyson walked in.

"Hello, I'm the Custom's Official and…"

"Did I ask you who the fuck you were?"

Unfazed by my interruption, he continued to talk with a voice that was much deeper and more masculine than Tyson's.

"What are you doing here in this country? Are you on business? Vacation?"

"Yes…business," I answered.

Aggravated.

Pissed.

Ready to fight.

"What kind of business are you on without suitcases?" he asked. He then eyed the bathing suit that I still had one. "Odd attire to be traveling…yeah?"

"Fuck you," I sarcastically spat. "None of my information is any of your *fucking* business, that's what kind of business I'm on, and that's where my bags are!"

He gazed at me, not moved by my smart comebacks, then continued. "We have reason to believe that you are trying to smuggle drugs out of this country. We will execute a strip search to ensure that's not the case."

He smirked, revealing that he had already begun the search in his mind, and I played into it by opening and closing my legs just like Sharon Stone had done in *Basic Instinct*. I'd managed to retie the sarong I had on around my body. Now it looked more like a little dress. I stood up and began to undress myself, taking everything off. Within seconds, I stood like a stripper preparing for the pole with nothing on and watched the print in his black uniform pants rise.

He was excited.

Really excited.

"I've been a really bad girl. Are you going to spank me?" I asked, as I leaned over on the table, exposing my huge ass. I spread my legs and rubbed my hands along the crack of my butt, making sure to graze my fingers along my pussy.

And then I slapped my ass.

Really, really hard.

"Spank me, Daddy," I said seductively, in a childlike voice. Those sick muthafuckas love when you change your voice to sound like an innocent child. Hopefully, all this bullshit would set me free. "Take out that big cock and stick it in my mouth to shut me the fuck up!"

I got up from my bending position and walked toward him. I dropped to my knees and reached for his zipper. The punk-ass Custom's Officer, who had so much to say a few minutes ago was now speechless, knowing he was about to get his dick sucked. I managed to squeeze his big dick through the small slit of his pants and rubbed it against my face.

"What will you do for Mommy if I let you stick it down my throat and choke me with it?"

"What do you want Daddy to do for you?" he asked, playing along with my game. It was at that moment that I knew I had him.

"I want Daddy to get me on that flight, so I can go home with my family." I licked the head of his peach stick and said, "I promise I'll be a good girl."

"Shut the fuck up and show me how good you'll be," he ordered.

He put his hand on the back of my head and forced his dick even further into my mouth, causing me to choke a bit. It had been a while since I'd given head and my reflexes proved it. My jaw muscles clearly weren't what they used to be, because I gagged every time he thrust deeper into my mouth. Not one to complain, I took hold of the situation by wrapping my hand around his meat to slow down his movements.

And then I fondled it.

Tickled his balls.

I found my rhythm, as my tongue swirled around his toy, making him flinch with every move I made. This head was going to get me on the plane. I knew it would.

It throbbed in my mouth, but worth it all. I could tell my freedom was just minutes away by the way his head titled backward, and pupils rolled to the back of his head, leaving only the color of white. Besides, his long, hard throbs let me know that he was about to explode any second. I pulled and yanked at it, causing a suction effect in my mouth. It was my time to shine. My time to break free. He moaned, squirmed a little, and with no ability to contain himself, he released his warm, creamy island babies all over my face. I wiped some of his nut off my eye and stuck it in my mouth for an added touch.

"Was I a good girl?" I asked, while licking the rest of his cum off my mouth.

"Stand up," he demanded.

He tucked his satisfied dick back into his pants and zipped swiftly.

"So now…I need to get on that flight. Are you letting me go?"

"I said get up!" he shouted, as his boss could be heard on the outside of the door.

The tone in his voice confused me.

It was harsh and authoritative. I stood up with his creamy juice still attached to my face and looked at him. He turned me around forcefully, slapped some handcuffs on me and proceeded to say, "You're under arrest for the assault of a Custom's Officer!"

Chapter Ten
(Oshyn)

"I saw her," I kept telling Brooklyn fearfully. He had just gotten comfortable in his seat and had closed his eyes. "I saw Chloe in the parking lot. Here at the airport, just as we were parking!"

"Oshyn, please, not now. Not right now!"

He rubbed his temples, trying to relieve whatever stress I was causing him. If he rubbed any harder, he would take the black off of his skin. I wanted to tell him about seeing Chloe when I first noticed her, but my lips wouldn't move. The lady crossing the street carelessly with her children had me spellbound. The thought of hitting those children was too much to bear. And as much as I hated to admit it, it seemed like my dead son was one of the children with her. I was frozen in place, wondering if my mind was playing tricks on me.

I stared at Brooklyn as his eyes remained closed. I knew he was frustrated. He grieved for both me and Tuff, but was probably sick of me. The plane had yet to take off and he wasn't too fond of the sky, so I was sure he wanted to go to sleep before we took off. *I knew he would never believe me*, I thought to myself.

"Baby...please, wake up for just a minute."

I nudged him softly on his arm while he shifted, trying to get me off of him. I knew my antics were becoming annoying, but crazy or not, I saw what I saw.

"What? What is it? Talk," Brooklyn finally said.

He sat his chair up, even though he wasn't suppose to have it down anyway, and looked in my eyes. He didn't have to say it. The sarcasm, anger and disappointment were written all over his face.

"Ladies and gentlemen, due to the weather, we have a slight delay in our initial takeoff. Please be patient. We'll be departing as soon as possible. Thank you for flying with International Air," one of the stewardesses announced.

"Don't stop talking now," he threatened, obviously beyond frustrated.

I shifted in my seat, regretting the fact that I had even brought this up, but I knew it needed to be discussed.

"Brooklyn, I know I've been acting a little crazy lately, but..."

"Please, I can't. My head hurts," he confessed, rubbing it again. "My mind...hurts. I can't take this crap right now, Oshyn!"

I gave him a stern look. "Crap?"

Right before I was getting ready to dig into his ass about how he was speaking to me, he reached into his pocket and handed me a bottle of pills.
Oddly, they had been prescribed to me, and I hadn't been to a doctor in months.

"Zoloft?" I asked, snatching the bottle out of his hand. "What are you doing with this?"

"Take them!" He snatched the bottle out of my hand then proceeded to open it. He titled the bottle and two pills fell into his palm. "Please...take them!"

"Fuck you, Brooklyn!" I said through clenched teeth, as I unfastened my seatbelt to sit with Bella and Mye, who were sitting across from us. I quickly took Mye out of Bella's lap and sat down in the empty seat next to her then made myself comfortable. From her heavy sigh, it was obvious that I was bothering her, but I could care less.

"What the hell is wrong with you?" I asked her, as I put Mye back to sleep.

"Nothin'," she replied, as she rocked her head to whatever music was playing in her earphones.

"Yeah, it better had been nothing."

I rolled my eyes.

Daring her to say something. Anything. But she wouldn't.

"Bella, hand me some tissue from out of your purse," I asked, trying to dig green stuff out of Mye's nose with my fingernail, but those monsters wouldn't budge. I turned back to Bella, who had her eyes closed, and saw that she was still rocking to whatever beat played in her head.

I was sure that she heard me, but didn't feel like arguing anymore. Not wanting to cause any drama on the plane, I bent down and stuck my hand up under her seat to grab her small hot pink Juicy bag. I sat it on my lap and unzipped it, only to find a condom sitting on top of all her mess. Without thinking twice, I yanked her earplugs out of her ears.

"What the fuck is this?" I held the package up to her face and waited for an explanation. I could care less who heard my foul language at that point.

"Why were you going through my stuff?" she asked, totally disregarding the fact that her nine year old ass was caught red handed with a fucking condom.

I held Mye close to my chest, as I took my right hand and wrapped it around her neck; of course doing my best to squeeze the life out of her as quietly as I could before anyone could stop me.

"Oshyn, what are you doing?" Brooklyn asked, as he rushed to pry my hands off of Bella.

I never noticed him get up. Never even noticed his huge frame standing over me. Bella coughed violently, and gasped for air.

"She's having sex, Brooklyn!" I held up the condom for

71

him to see, while he managed to take Mye out of my hands.

"Shhhh! You're making too much noise!" someone said a few rows back.

I ignored them. Never even looked back to see who'd said it. Was handling family business and that took priority. We were only four rows from the back, so there weren't many people around us.

"But you tried to kill her," Brooklyn whispered sadly.

"She's nine years old and she's having sex!" I yelled. "Do something about it! Oh, wait…since she's not your daughter, you don't have to reprimand her, is that it?"

"Lower your voice," he warned.

I peered over the seat and realized that we had attracted some unwanted attention from the nosey people that sat around us.

"Don't *nobody* give a fuck about these people! Fuck you *and* fuck them!"

"Handle your problems at home, lady…this is a public place," someone else in the front of me yelled.

"The very next person who decides to say anything to me or my family will get dealt with," I warned.

Another woman joined in on the attack against me, and just when I was about to go off on her, I noticed someone getting on the plane. Although we were sitting closer to the back of the huge airbus I was still able to get a glimpse of who it was.

"Chloe?" I said out loud to no one in particular. The mouths of the passengers were still moving, but I didn't notice anything. Just watched as the woman I saw in the parking lot take a seat in first class. "She's here. Chloe's on the plane!" I whispered to Brooklyn. Instantly, my body began to shiver, and goose bumps popped up all over my arms. "I gotta get off of here!" I shouted.

"I'm sorry, but is there a problem over here?" the stewardess asked, blocking the view of my sister.

"Brooklyn, she's here. She's on the plane!" I screamed even louder.

I needed him to respond.

Needed him to take me serious.

To say anything other than the loud screams of nothing that escaped from his mouth.

"No, there's nothing going on here," Brooklyn told the stewardess calmly. "My wife was just about to take her medication. She gets like this right before flying," he lied.

Brooklyn tried to spare himself the embarrassment of telling her the truth; that his wife was going insane and there was nothing he could do about it. I ignored him, and began devising a plan to make my way up to the front. I had to see for myself if it was really her or not.

"Both of you move out of my way. I'm going to see my sister." As I proceeded to get up out of my seat, my intent to walk forward was blocked by Brooklyn's chest. "Move!"

"Sit down," he warned.

"Get...out...of...my...way!" I demanded.

He took his hand and threw me back in my seat like I was a child. Like I was one of his children. Like I couldn't make my own decisions. I heard a few cheers from the crowd, then turned to give them all dirty looks.

"I will put both of you off the plane if she doesn't calm down, sir," the stewardess informed." She was obviously at her wits end, and even though I could tell she didn't want to, I was leaving her no choice but to be stern.

Brooklyn spoke with fire in his voice, "Don't worry, it won't happen again. I have it all under con..."

"Fuck you, bitch! You're just trying to keep me away from my sister just like everyone else. But you won't succeed this time. I will kill you before I let you keep me from her. I'll kill you!" I screamed.

"That's it," the stewardess warned, right before walking to the front of the plane. "I'm not putting up with this anymore. She's out of here."

Chapter Eleven
(Chloe)

With several feet over the threshold of the plane, a sigh of relief filled my senses. It seemed as if every passenger awaited my arrival. Here I was in trouble, had just sucked a crusty dick, and still got the red carpet treatment. The anorexic looking stewardess moved swiftly, telling me the only space for my oversized pocketbook was in the open compartment where she stood. I felt like I had no choice as I heard the captain announce that we were now ready to depart.

"You're in seat 3A," the stewardess announced in her French accent.

I chuckled. "Ain't this a bitch, first class. Umph, I'm the shit," I boasted to myself.

I shot the skinny, white bitch a grin and threw my purse in the air to store up top. Mid-air I realized how much other luggage was in the container and I struggled for second to squeeze mine in. That was until a tall gentleman stood up to assist me.

I froze.

It must've been fate.

It was the same guy I'd seen brush past me when I was fussing to get on the plane. As he moved my way I got a whiff of his good smelling cologne, glanced at his tall, slender frame, and attractive bald head. It was shiny, sexy, and simply needed me to rub it for perfection.

There were only about five other people in first class, so I held my composure and just nodded my thanks when he touched my hand to help. My first thought was, *damn, this is it*!

He's the one.

All six foot four of him.

Luck was surely on my side for the day. First, I managed to talk my way out of being put in jail by threatening the Custom's guy that I would tell his boss the truth. I told that idiot that I'd held some of his semen in my mouth and spit it into my bra for evidence. His faggot ass believed me and agreed to get me on the plane if I kept my mouth shut. Secondly, meeting Mr. Right on the plane, and realizing he was in seat 3C was just like hitting the lottery.

As soon as I sat down chills flew through my body. His smell mesmerized me to the point that I was afraid to look him in the face. I couldn't help but think back to the old lady. She'd said, "Tall and dark with plenty of money." My fellow passenger was definitely tall and slender, and reminded me of Michael Jordan, just a few shades darker. He was sexy, well kept, and dressed like he was making some serious paper. He asked me if I had enough space because he would move to another seat nearby if I wanted to stretch out.

"Oh no, I'm fine," I said with ease. On the real, I wanted to jump over into his seat and jam my tongue down his throat.

It was official. I was smitten like a school girl being manipulated by an older man. He was flipping through a Black Enterprise Magazine, while I eyed him like a correctional officer watching an inmate. His twenty thousand dollar Cartier watch had me captivated. It was an edition that had been featured in Forbes, all blinged out, and that Tommy had told me about. Personally, I'd never had the pleasure of experiencing anything special edition for my wrist, yet a mental note was made to get his and hers soon.

It had my nipples cold and hard, wondering how many carats sat around the diamond encrusted bezel. Then there was the one diamond stud in his left ear. It had to have been three carats, a VVS stone, I was sure.

I wanted him.

Badly.

I was willing to do anything.

The two by two bathroom was fine.

The seat that we sat in would have been better.

My eyes seemed to dart away every time he caught me looking at him. As soon as I felt the plane descending into the air, I lifted my window to take a look at the clouds. It was my hope that the serene scene would take my mind off Jordan's twin. But within seconds, he sucked me in even more.

In his northern accent he started and wouldn't stop. "So, was your trip business or pleasure?"

I tried to speak…just couldn't. I was tongue tied and kept my eyes on his bright white teeth. "Ahhhhhh…"

He smiled even more. "Are you thinking about your man or something?" he asked.

I knew the accent was Jersey or New York, so I thought of something else to say. "I'm single, but used to date a guy from Jersey. That's where you're from, right?"

"Nah, Manhattan actually," he corrected, showing me every dimple he had.

"So, tell me, what do you do?" I asked him suspiciously.

"A little of this and that." He paused. "And you?"

"Big things. Things you could never imagine." I smiled.

"Word."

He crossed his legs, letting his crisp pant leg drape over his gators. Everything he wore appeared to be top notch; even the custom-made button down shirt with the initials C.M.

"So, what's C.M stand for?"

He extended his hand. "Pardon my manners. Carlos Manning," he said. "And you are?"

"Chloe." I paused. I thought about saying Chloe Manning, but wasn't sure if he'd appreciate the humor. "Chloe Rodriguez," I finally said then smiled.

"Well, Chloe Rodriguez, tell me a little about yourself. We've got a long ride." He rested his head back on the seat. "I would ask how your day was, but I will say that it's safe to say you spent your time swimming?" And then he laughed.

"Cute. Real cute," I replied, returning his humorous gesture. His eyes that roamed up and down my body let me know that he was referring to my bathing suit. Something that was totally inappropriate for this type of travel. "I was in a rush. Didn't have time to change."

Just then the commotion from the back of the plane started again. It was the same annoying commotion that had been going on when I first got on the plane. My lust for Carlos had side-tracked me then, but shit was getting louder.

All of a sudden, a chubby, dark-skinned stewardess brushed Carlos as she came bolting down the aisle. She rushed over to Miss Anorexia, complaining. "I got her name, Oshyn Jones," she read from a small piece of ripped paper. "She's traveling with two kids and her husband," she snapped. "He's trying to calm her down and it's not working if you ask me." She paused, placing her hands on her hips and ended with a huge huff. "What should I do?"

"I mean we're about to depart, what can you do now?" Miss Anorexic said, rolling her eyes. "I don't feel like dealing with that now. I wanna get in the air. Let's just leave it alone. I'm sure her husband will be able to calm her down."

I couldn't help but to wonder what kind of scene Oshyn was making that was causing this kind of uproar. She was normally the one to remain calm, but everyone seemed to be aggravated by her presence. *Maybe she told Brooklyn about seeing me in the parking lot*, I thought to myself. *Maybe she saw me get on the plane.*

Abruptly, I cleared my throat. "Excuse me…but as a

paying passenger, it's annoying," I interjected.

Carlos took charge. "Just close the curtains, that should do the trick," he said with confidence.

My thought was to talk shit and press the situation hard with tons of complaints. But I didn't want to buck Carlos. His smoothness had everyone in awe, even had both stewardess eating from the palm of his hand. The heavy-set one closed the curtain, separating first class from coach, while I thought maliciously about my next comment.

"Where's the plane marshal? I mean…or at least a confined compartment for people like that?" My hands were spread apart and my temper had risen, almost forgetting Carlos was watching me. "Damn! I paid a lot of money for this first class seat. And there's no class at all on this plane!"

I stopped.

Caught myself.

I was back to the real Chloe.

Carlos looked at me with surprise. "So, you're a naughty girl, huh?"

"No, not really. I'm so sorry," I pleaded. "I just hate chaos, and that passenger shouting and acting crazy is getting to me." I paused to put my puppy dog face on. "You see, mental illness runs in my family."

"Word," he said sympathetically.

Instantly I got wet. His concerned voice, mixed with the roughness of how he spoke, turned me on. He had class, yet had a ruggedness to him. "At least three people in my family died at the hands of mental illness."

"So sorry to hear that, but the good thing is you're fine. And I do mean fine."

He grinned.

"So, how old are you?" I asked curiously.

"How old do I look?" he shot back.

I melted into the seat as he made love to me with his eyes. "Ahhhh twenty-eight?"

"Thirty-one," he admitted.

"You look good."

"Not as good as you," he said, licking his supple lips. Without warning, he moved over to the empty middle seat between us. "Mind if I get a little closer?" Carlos asked.

I simply beamed then spread my legs. "I like a man who takes charge."

Carlos looked shocked.

And I wanted to remain a lady so we could start our relationship the right way. I decided to take things slow, so I grabbed his oversized palm that held the large diamond and placed it directly under my sarong. His hand felt warm, soothing, almost as if it belonged on my pussy.

And had found its home.

He knew what I wanted.

The question was could he give it to me without anyone noticing? Hell, we had an eight hour flight back to the states. I imagined I would cum three or four times by then.

Chapter Twelve
(Chloe)

At the hotel.

Getting fucked.

Tuff's funeral wasn't for another two days, so I had some time to spare until I had to get down to business. There was no rush since Brooklyn and Oshyn weren't going to leave town until his cousin was buried. I had time to have a little fun. Fun I deserved.

"The real Chloe is back," I told myself, puffing on a *woo* given to me by Carlos. To my surprise, it was a blunt mixed with weed and cocaine. I had never smoked a woo before. Guess the hospital kept me from being up on things. Oddly, it calmed my nerves and helped me focus on his slick ass. Hell, he was hitting me with all kinds of surprises. The nigga was into everything I thought he wouldn't be into. His business attire and confident swagger had me fooled. Everything about Carlos was now starting to surprise me.

When I first met him on the plane, his demeanor told me he was stuck up, suave and debonair. Instead, I'd hooked up and fell in love with an undercover thug. He dressed the part of a businessman daily, but on the real, the nigga was hood. Of course, I liked it like that. Hood mixed with plenty of money. *What could be better?* I asked myself, with my legs spread wide open on the king-sized bed.

Carlos stood above me, caressing my bare thighs and throwing out words that got me horny again. "You want some more of big Dick Willie," he taunted, grabbing his shit.

"C'mere, Los," I called over to him.

He turned his back and slipped on his crisp slacks, letting me know our fuck fest had to stop. We had already pounded our way through three rounds of sex, yet my pussy continued to pulsate, telling me it wanted more of Carlos. Everything about him felt right; the way he talked, the way he moved, and the way he handled his business on the phone. I felt like yanking Carlos by his tie back onto the bed, but I knew he had to go. His big show would start at nine tonight, and the artist were expected to arrive for a sound check at three o'clock.

"So, what time you coming to my show?" he asked, rushing over to me and bending down to kiss his sweet pussy.

I lay back on the bed with my head resting against the headboard, unable to answer. I simply moaned, closed my eyes and let his wet lips make love to my clit.

Abruptly, he stopped, but I yanked his baldhead back toward the treasure.

"Come here," I begged. "Eat it, pleaseeeeeee. Just one more time."

"I can't, Chloe," he laughed slightly. "Tonight, I got you after the show. I gotta go meet up with the sound company. They need their paper." He kissed at me through the air. "You know I got a lot of money riding on this show."

All I heard was blah, blah, blah. I was use to getting everything my way, and I wanted him *now*.

"So, what's in it for me?" I asked, pulling him by the collar. I lifted my body and pushed myself toward him. We met eye to eye, with Carlos still on his feet, leaning my way.

"Yo, tonight, I'll bring the profits back to the hotel room and we'll fuck all night."

I got excited.

"On top of the money, right?" I asked excitedly.

I loosened my grip, noticing Carlos squirming to get away.

"Word is bond."

"And we upgrading to a suite tonight, right?"

"No doubt," he said with confidence. "Anything you want, you get."

I smiled widely inside and damn near came. Those words were music to my ears.

"I'll be there by ten. I got front row seats, right?" I asked, as he slipped his pistol into a cuff underneath the bottom of his pant leg.

He grinned. "Only the best for my lady," he uttered, walking toward the hotel door.

I smiled back, wondering how the hell I landed his chocolate ass. "Love you!" I shouted.

The door slammed and I rolled over like a dog in heat, thinking about how my life was about to change. I knew I would soon be a housewife, so I had to change up my wardrobe. A few presentable pieces wouldn't hurt just in case he needed me to accompany him on business. I needed to get my hair done, and most importantly, I needed to get on the internet in the lobby to find us a place to live when we returned to Manhattan.

Carlos traveled a lot, but it would be my job to make our home comfy and cozy for his return. He told me that three to four times per month he left the city to make his bread. Doing shows was his only livelihood. It was how he made his millions...a gracious living. From what he revealed, he'd been mixed up in some illegal money making shit a few years back where he made a lot of cash, and pretty much gave him start up money to become a big time promoter.

That's where the whole gun thing came in. He needed it. Said some folks were after him. Wanted to see him dead. I wasn't worried because Carlos was about his word. Plus, he'd told me a few stories about things he'd done in the past.

People he'd shot. Dudes he'd stabbed. And haters he'd disposed of. The thought of my man sent chills up and down my spine. Then the interruption came.

It was him.

My supplemental check.

Old ass Tommy.

"Yes!" I answered like a raging bull on the second ring.

"Chloe, I've been calling you." Tommy sounded like a weak lamb.

"Oh really," I countered, showing that I didn't give a fuck.

He sighed heavily. "You got the money I sent on Tuesday?"

"Yeah, I got it." I smacked my lips and remained silent, hoping he would get angry and hang up.

His next words sent me into oblivion.

"I need to see you soon. I'll even come to Rochester," he uttered. "I…I…I changed my will like we discussed." He paused hesitantly. "But I need to see you before I turn it in to my lawyer. There are a few important things we gotta discuss."

My eyeballs rolled to the back of my head, and dollar signs replaced my brown pupils. I couldn't speak. Could barely even move. How honored. Tommy wanted me to now be the beneficiary of the majority of his belongings. His estate, which we already discussed back in the hospital, was worth more than three million dollars. It would be a stretch having him come to Rochester, but I had no other choice.

"Chloe, are you there?" he asked worriedly.

"I'm here."

"I know you're there for your brother's funeral so stay put. I'm coming there. The will has to be changed immediately."

I sensed the urgency in his voice. His voice was a bit weaker than before. Sounded like death was knocking on his door a lot faster than we both had anticipated. I braced my-

84

self to act concerned for the first time.

"Is everything okay?"

"Not really. I'll explain when I get there. I'll call for our meeting spot when I get off the plane. I'll have to come right back, so we'll meet near the airport."

"Bet," I said then hung up to fabricate my plan.

At ten o'clock sharp, I found myself in the green room backstage, rubbing elbows with the elite. The room was small, intimate, and laced with two tables carrying the finest wines, fruits, bottles of liquor, and at the headliners request, Remy Martin VSOP. I stood in the corner watching Ludacris' manager shout the do's and don'ts of how things were to go down, but my man handled it all. He was sharp with his words, even though the sweat could be seen across his forehead.

Suddenly, nasty thoughts entered my mind as I watched Carlos give instructions to a few more of his workers. "I need it done right," I heard him say, then saw two chicks in the corner snicker his way.

Before I knew it, I'd gotten closer to them. They were two of ten people in the lowly lit room, and laughed secretly in a corner, as if they were making comments about us all. The music played low inside, sounding as if it was coming from a hidden Ipod, but it didn't keep me from hearing the word *flunkie*.

They both turned as I got up on them. The dominant, mouthy looking bitch just glared when I asked if the champagne had arrived yet.

"I'm not sure," she responded, after giving me a dirty look. "And you are?"

"Oh, I'm none of your fucking business." I extended my hand. "I'm with my fiancé. Just making sure everything is okay."

They both looked at me like I was stuck on stupid.

"Carlos," I announced. "I'm with Carlos."

They burst into laughter.

"Well, I'm Sheila and this is Tyese. We're with D-Rock. He's opening for Luda. And, honey, we know all about Carlos." They laughed again.

Sheila had on a short strapless leather dress, three inch stilettos, and a bad weave all down her back. It was clear she thought she was hot shit by the way she flipped me off with her eyes. Her girl paid more attention to my expression, and knew I wasn't to be fucked with.

I folded my arms tightly across my torso, and told them that I thought I'd overheard them saying something about my man.

"I just want to be clear, if something is said about him, say it to me." I was firm with my tone, but quiet enough to keep our bitter conversation under wraps.

"You don't know, do you?" Sheila asked innocently.

"Know what?" I asked.

My expression puzzled them both, but I refused to let them know they had caught me off guard. So, I just hit them with some confident words. "I know all that I need to know."

"Oh, I'm sure," Sheila mocked, flipping her weave in the process.

The song *Stand By Your Man* played in my mind. *Fuck these haters,* I told myself, as the M.C. for the show announced throughout the arena. At the same time my phone rang.

I felt trapped.

It was Tommy.

Didn't want to leave, but that money was calling. The D-Rock bitches shook their heads sympathetically as they watched me talk in codes, then turned to leave the room.

"Nice meeting you," Sheila stated in a mocking tone.

"Oh, I'll be back. And you will see me again." I hit her with a fake smile, and jetted out the green room, hoping Carlos wouldn't notice that I was gone. I knew I had less than an

86

hour to make it back. I figured the show would be going on and he wouldn't miss me anyway.

As soon as I stepped into the revolving door of the Hilton by the airport fifteen minutes later, my adrenaline was in over-drive. The lobby was full of people quickly moving back and forth. For ten-thirty at night it was busier than I'd expected. I kept looking around for Tommy, and had even checked the bar, when I finally noticed him sitting alone near the fireplace in the lobby. The area he'd chosen was cozy; two high back comfy chairs, and a stool and table placed neatly between.

"Hey, Tommy," I said excitedly, walking up on him.

He could barely turn his stiff neck as he greeted me in a depressed tone.

His situation was serious. I could feel it. He looked even older than before. Almost fragile. Like two minutes from his deathbed. "You feeling okay?" I asked.

Tommy cleared his throat then coughed. "Not really," he revealed, then coughed again like he suffered from a bad case of Emphysema, the smoker's disease.

"Look, I'll go into details later." He stopped to take a deep breath. "My daughter is coming in town tomorrow, and I wanted to get this business straight with you."

My face was already bawled up before he could finish his sentence. "Your daughter? I thought you said she didn't want you in her life. You said you hadn't seen her in ten years."

"I hadn't, Chloe. But she called. And honestly, I'm not doing well. So, I wanted you to have a copy of my will. You know how things go when people die." He paused then looked at me like he loved me for real. "My daughter is my blood. She'll get everything by law if you don't sign these papers."

Judging by the way Tommy pulled the papers from the large brown envelope, I knew I'd be a multi-millionaire soon. He moved like he was one hundred years old, as he flipped through the stack. His hands seemed to be peeling and wrinkled, but I rubbed them any way before going into my purse.

"How's your daughter?" he asked me out of the blue.

Luckily, he didn't look me in the face. He was busy trying to find the spots where I needed to sign. "Oh, she's getting better. Thanks to you." I smiled.

I pulled out one of Carlos' Black and Milds and kicked my foot up on the stool. I just shook my head back and forth as I lit up. I couldn't believe how Tommy was deteriorating.

He needed a coffin to rest in.

Bad.

I got so caught up into staring that I didn't hear him rushing me for a signature. He said he wanted to hurry so he could catch the last flight out, eleven twenty-five to be exact. I wanted him gone too. He coughed uncontrollably, trying to get his next words out.

"Chloe, sign here for now. I'll get you copies as soon as I turn this into my lawyer. I think we should move in together when you get back."

I swallowed hard. "Just give me time to get my daughter straight." Then I stood, kissed him on the cheek, and told him I loved him.

"I love you, too, Chloe. Just know you're the best thing that ever happened to me." He stopped to cough again. "I'll call you tomorrow, I gotta catch this flight."

Hell, I gotta get back to my man, I told myself. The bitches are probably all over him by now. I rushed out of the hotel doing thirty with my feet.

Chapter Thirteen

(Chloe)

Knock…knock…knock!

"Who is it?" Carlos screamed to the unwanted visitor that was pounding on our hotel room door. Although it was going on ten o'clock in the morning, we had just fallen asleep from counting all of the money *we* had made at the show last night. The sun was no match for the blinds, as not a speck of light had peeked through to the room. It was dark as night in here.

"Room service," the female voice said in an irritated, deep Spanish accent. She had a job to do and we were messing up her flow, or my guess was she had seen some nice pieces she wanted to steal and we had gotten in the way of her plans. Either way, she was out of luck.

"Go away!" Carlos demanded, as he turned over to face me. He took his hands and pulled me closer to his naked chocolate brown body, and then he kissed me on my forehead right before drifting back off to sleep. I closed my eyes in an attempt to follow in his steps, but there was no way I could do the same.

I still couldn't get the hundreds of thousands of dollars that took us hours to count out of my mind. I could still smell the sweet scent of currency, so much of it that it made me

sick. So much of the dirty money that my fingertips had
turned dingy. So much of it that I was never going to let this
dude get away, because this was different. He trusted me.
Never for once thinking that I would set him up. And for the
first time in my life, the thought never crossed my mind.

I was use to getting money. Big money. Long money. I
had traveled all around the world in private jets and custom
yachts, but nothing compared to this. Simple and pure love.
The great sex we had and the chemistry that we shared
made all of this money an added bonus. I couldn't figure out
what had gotten into me, but this love thing was a feeling
that I could learn to get use to.

Now, I had to choose between Carlos and Brooklyn, a
choice that would disappoint one of them deeply if it wasn't
them, but I decided to worry about that later. Carlos was
here, in the flesh, with his arms wrapped around me. Feeling
safe, I dozed off.

"Babe," I heard a voice say, as a soft tug came on my
shoulder. "Baby, are you going to sleep all day? Wake up!"

The tug got a little harder.

Turned into shoves.

I peeked my head out of the fluffy white comforter,
only to be greeted by the scent of eggs, bacon and grits, and
then I realized that Carlos was no longer lying by my side.

"What time is it?" I asked, not really wanting to be
bothered. It felt like I had only been asleep for a few minutes,
and I had no intention on waking up. I was extremely tired.

"It's almost one o'clock…wake up!" Carlos said, as he
snatched the cover off of me. I got an immediate attitude and
snatched it back, placing it over my body, where it initially
was. "I brought you breakfast in bed, so you need to get up
and eat it."

My stomach growled and my bladder felt like it was

going to burst, but I was too exhausted to move. I felt like if I could just go back to sleep, I wouldn't feel the hunger pains, and the explosion of my bladder would just be an after-thought. So I closed my eyes and tried to ignore his constant words, but none of it seemed to work.

"Chloe, wake your ass up!" Carlos shouted.

I opened my eyes just enough to watch him walk over to the window and pull the curtains open, letting the incredi-bly bright sunlight in. I nestled back under the covers like a vampire, trying to avoid being burnt to dust.

"Are you serious? Why can't you just leave me alone?" I pleaded with him.

"Because you can sleep when you're dead, that's why. If you're going to be with me, you'll learn quickly that sleep is not a luxury that we can afford. I barely sleep. There is just too much money to make. Too much money to spend."

Now he was talking my language.

He pulled the cover off of me again, and this time I let him, exposing my bare body against the crisp white sheets. It took my eyes a while to adjust to the daylight, as I reached over and grabbed a piece of crunchy bacon from off the plate.

"I'm up now!" I announced with an attitude, as I took a bite of the meat. "What do you have planned for the day?"

He was already fully dressed in a pair of Hugo Boss jeans and a red Lacoste polo. He grabbed the suitcase full of money and put it on the bed, unzipped it, and took bundles of money out of it, spreading it all over my body.

He took his hands and pried my legs apart, exposing my thick pink pussy. My nipples stood firmly up and pointed in his direction, letting him know that they were ready to be sucked on. Letting him know that I was ready to be sucked on.

I swallowed the last piece of bacon down as he kissed my treasure. The urge that I had to pee was quickly replaced with the urge I had to nut all over his face. Then, without warning, he slid the tip of his tongue directly into my asshole, making me jump. Making me cum before I wanted to. It felt so good that I couldn't hold it in any longer.

"Wow, that was fast," he said, as he saw the flow of happiness that seemed to pour non-stop out of my pussy. He smiled at me with the happy juice glazed over his face, and with ass juice glazed over his tongue. *Yeah, this is going to work out great,* I thought, as he went to the bathroom to clean himself off. What I loved more than anything else was a nasty nigga, and I had one in my possession. I finished up the breakfast, which had turned cold, and swallowed the last piece of egg when he came out of the bathroom.

He got a little closer and touched my hair with his fingertips, and as he worked his way down to my ear, I jumped. I moved his hand and turned my head away before he had the opportunity to notice that one of my ears were fake.

"Why don't you like when I touch you there?" he asked, noticing that this wasn't the first time that I had moved his hand.

"My ears are sensitive," I lied. "Never really liked anyone playing around them." Just like a man, he shrugged his shoulders and dismissed my pet peeve.

"You never even told me what happened to your face?"

I didn't know what to say. Just ignored him until he continued.

"Well, get up and get dressed," he said to me, as he began putting the money back into the suitcase. "We're going to Toronto today. I want to do some shopping, maybe even hit up some casinos."

As tempting as that sounded, my focus immediately went to Oshyn. She was the real reason that I was even in the city, and I didn't want to lose focus of that fact. I was never one to let a man take me off my game, but with Carlos, I was making an exception. Just as I was about to tell him that I couldn't go with him, I quickly remembered the fact that Oshyn came for the funeral too, and wouldn't leave until her husband's cousin was buried. So, if nothing else, that bought

92

me some time. Toronto was only a two hour trip from Rochester, so I could make it back in no time. I got up and got dressed like I was told.

It was a little after three in the afternoon, and the two hour drive flew by quicker than I thought as we reached our destination. Toronto, Canada. I hadn't been there since I left Rochester and moved to Raleigh, but it was still beautiful. An exact replica of Manhattan, New York, with all the five star restaurants and hotels to match.

"Where do you want to go first?" he asked, letting me know that the ball was in my court. That today was my day. That everyday would always be my day.

"Put Bloor Street West in the navigation," I instructed him. "That's where I want to go first."

This was one of Toronto's Fifth Avenue and Rodeo Drive look alike streets, which housed some of the most expensive boutiques. It took us only about ten minutes to get there from where we were, and I immediately got excited like a child on Christmas Day. It had been way too long since money was at my disposal, and I just couldn't contain myself. I started to hyperventilate.

"There! There! Pull over there!" I demanded. Once I laid my eyes on the Hermes boutique, all of my worries went away. I practically hopped out of the car before it stopped rolling and Carlos took care of the valet dude. When all of that was settled, he grabbed my hand and led me into the doorway of pure heaven.

"Good afternoon," an older woman said to me in a French accent. I forgot that in Canada they spoke French, but then again, I thought to myself, *who the fuck cares*? Her jet black hair carried a single white strip in the middle, and she wore a black nicely tailored suit. Probably St. John. She was very polished.

"Hey," I replied back, as I brushed passed her to get my hands on one of the bags. I didn't really want to entertain small talk. My goal was to just get in and get out as fast as I could so that we could get back to Rochester. Trying to mix business with pleasure.

Carlos followed behind me like a lost puppy as I bounced from counter to counter, trying to see which one I wanted to take home. They all seemed to reach out for me, begging me to take them. And then I spotted it. The one that caught my attention and never let it go.

"That one," I said to the woman, pointing her in the direction in which I was talking about. She took a long glance at the purse I was referring to and then at me.

"Ummm, yes. That particular style is sixty-five thousand dollars. Perhaps I can show you where our five thousand dollar Hermes bags are."

It seemed like time stood still, as I felt the anger in me slowly rise to the top, like lava in a volcano, ready to erupt at any second. I took a moment to re-evaluate what I looked like to make her say that bullshit to me. My jeans were Rock and Republic, and I had on a short sleeve silk Alice and Olivia blouse. A pair of Tory Burch flats adorned my feet, and my hair was bouncy and in perfect place. No diamonds dripped off my ears, my neck, my wrist, or my fingers like they did once before, but I was going to make sure that that would never happen again. The jewelry store would be our next stop. I couldn't afford to be mistaken for an average bitch again.

"Come, let me show you where they are," the saleslady insisted, as she unknowingly knocked me out of my daydream back into reality.

"You dumb bitch, I know exactly what I said! Take the fucking bag that I asked you for down now!" I snapped.

I startled her.

Could tell in the way she paused that she was frozen in fear.

I opened my mouth to let her have some more, when I

94

felt Carlos' warm touch on my shoulder, letting me know that he would handle the rest.

It reminded me of the *Pretty Woman* movie, where Richard Gere took control.

"I'm sure you just misheard her," Carlos told the lady, giving her the benefit of the doubt. "She said that she wanted to see *this* bag, not the cheap ones that you're trying to lead her to."

"Oh, okay…yeah…yeah, I mean yes, of course," she stuttered, as she scuffled to get back to the item I had originally requested.

She took it out of the case and handed me the black crocodile skin Birkin bag. The hardware was plated in fourteen carat gold, and this particular one had diamonds encrusted on the buckle.

"I want this," I notified her.

Carlos took stacks of hundreds out of his bag and sat them on the table. The amount of money equaled out to the cost of the bag plus the tax, but we got a bit of a discount since our money was worth more over here than it was in the states. She went to prepare to bag it up, when I let her know that I would be carrying it out as is.

"But of course, Mrs…Mrs...I'm sorry, I didn't get your name," she admitted, as we began to walk away.

"Fuck off, bitch," were the last words she heard me say as we left the building.

"Damn, my baby is expensive," Carlos said, as he took a closer look at his sixty-five thousand dollar investment. "I need to start making more money to be with you," he joked.

And he was right.

This was just the beginning.

"Where to next?" he asked, allowing me to lead the way, and I knew just the spot, a diamond boutique that would make Elizabeth Taylor proud, Royal de Versailles.

We didn't have to walk far because it was right next door to Hermes, and when we entered, we were greeted with nothing but smiles. *Must be the bag*, I concluded to my-self, as everyone had a hard time keeping their eyes off of it.

"You have impeccable taste," a guy sitting behind the counter said to me.

"Thank you," I said back, finally glad that someone was able to appreciate class when they saw it.

"You're a diamond, girl," he continued, laying the flat-tery on as thick as he could. I assumed that he had been doing this for a while, or he knew a bad bitch when he saw one. Either way his words were music to my ears.

"I need it all," I confessed. "Earrings, bracelet..."

"And what about a ring?" he said, directing that question to Carlos.

Assuming that he would stutter at the sight of pres-sure, Carlos proved me wrong by just smiling and smoothly saying, "Whatever she wants."

I had found my Big Poppa!

The jeweler had me trying on all the flawless pieces, and at least an hour went by before I found the right ones. A six carat pair of diamond earrings hung off my ears, while a five carat tear drop necklace was draped around my neck. A studded out Cartier watch adorned my wrist, and the four-teen carat forty-eight thousand dollar princess cut ring that Carlos picked out, sparkled on my finger.

"How long have you two been together?" the jeweler asked, as he worked to put everything back in its place. Tempted to tell him a lie, that we had been together for sev-eral years, I opted to instead tell the truth.

"It's only been two days since we met," I said proudly.

"Nice," he said with a smile on his face. "Must be something in the air, because you're like the third couple I've come across that have come in and said that they met less than a month ago. Guess that love at first sight thing is real, huh?"

"Yeah," Carlos and I said at the same time.

"Well, that beautiful piece you're wearing on your fin-ger certainly says so."

96

"That's just a promise ring," Carlos told him. "The real thing will be bigger and better."

He paid for my things and we said our goodbyes as we made our way back outside.

"I'm pretty hungry," I told him. Didn't really want to stop shopping to eat, but I hadn't had anything except for the cold breakfast earlier in the day, and I was beginning to get weak.

"Me too," he said, as he handed the valet our ticket stub. We waited hand in hand, playfully kissing on one another as we waited for our car to come.

"Thank you," I said, surprising myself. Never would've thought that sincere sweet things would have come out of my mouth, but for the last couple of days, I actually meant what I said.

"You deserve it," was all he said back as the car pulled up. After we got in, he fastened his seatbelt and asked, "Where do you want to eat at?"

Instead of driving around aimlessly on an empty stomach, I decided to ask the young valet guy for some suggestions. I cracked the window and got his attention.

"We need some place to eat. An expensive place," I added, letting him know what kind of taste I had.

"You will like Lai Wah Heen. It's the celebrity and millionaire hot spot in Toronto, and that's because they're the only ones that can afford it."

After he gave us the directions, we drove off and enjoyed the scenery as we tried to stay on the path the valet gave us.

"We've spent two days together," he reminded me. "I've *never* done this before with *any* woman. It makes me feel kind of crazy, but it seems like we're supposed to be together."

I smiled.

Took all his words in.

"Do you have any children?" I asked, not wanting to prolong the question any further. "A wife, girlfriend, bitch on

97

the side?"

"Nothing. No kids, wife, girl, nothing. Making money has kept me from all of those luxuries, that's why I'm so surprised that I'm with you. This is some shit I wouldn't have even gotten myself into. I'm way too busy for it. What about you?"

"I'm just getting out of a relationship," I confessed. It was going to be hard to have to make a choice between him and Brooklyn, but if the gypsy was right, the choice was going to have to be made.

"Lucky me," he said as he smiled.

"Yeah, lucky you."

We pulled up at a red light and he leaned over to kiss me. Took the palm of his hand and tried brushing my hair out of my face, exposing my ear. I jumped. Swatted his hand away.

"What's wrong, why do you keep doing that?" he asked.

I looked at him and then out my window. My beauty was all I had to get me through in life, it was the only thing I had left of my mother's legacy. And now, some of it had faded away. I was still beautiful, but the scars I had made me question my appearance. The ear that was cut off and replaced with a fake was just too much to bear. Something I didn't want to share with someone else, especially not a man.

"I see your scars," he admitted. "And I don't care what they look like or how you got them. You're beautiful, and I'm happy that I met you. Your heart, your insecurities, and your mind are all safe with me. I promise."

The light turned green and he drove off. For the first time in my life I felt safe with a man. Totally safe.

"I'm going to get a room at the Westin," he said, as we weaved in and out of traffic. "We'll finish shopping today, relax, and head back to Rochester in the morning."

"No," I blurted out. "Um, I mean, I have to handle something important. Not that this isn't, but…"

"Hey, whatever you want," he said calmly. "Whatever you want."

I had to get back to Oshyn, and I refused to be tempted to stay with him any longer. As much as I wanted to, a job needed to be done. I unzipped his pants and dug his big dick from out of his boxers. Stroked it with my hands to get it rock hard and bent down to wrap my lips around it.

Sucked it until he squirmed in his seat.

Sucked it until my jaws hurt.

Sucked it until we pulled into the parking lot of the restaurant.

Until he came.

Until all his juice filled my mouth.

Until we were both satisfied.

Chapter Fourteen
(Oshyn)

Church to most people is a symbol for love.
Peace.
Happiness.
But church to me is a symbol for death.

Because this is where I came to say my goodbyes to too many people who carried pieces of my heart. To too many people who died before their time. To too many people I wished were still here.

I shifted from side to side as I tried getting a comfortable position on the hard wooden pew at Tuff's funeral service. The seats were so worn that if I wasn't careful, a splinter might have pierced my skin. I secretly wished there was somewhere else I could be. Wishing I had more family that I could go and visit. Wishing I didn't feel so alone.

My mind continued to play tricks on me, as I wondered what happened to Chloe when she got off the plane. It was if she'd just disappeared. There was no amount of convincing Brooklyn could do to me that would make me think any differently. I saw her with my own eyes, and I knew for a fact that that was her. By the time we got off the flight, she was gone. Without a trace, which had become her M.O.

Forced to be in the second row, Brooklyn and Bella

sat next to me as I rocked Mye in my arms. I was afraid that the spirit of death I had become accustomed to would snatch him out of my grasp, so I held my baby close to my breasts, refusing to lose him also.

We were all dressed in black. I had on a basic tight scoop neck dress that one would see Jackie O in. Something simple for the occasion. I also wore a small black hat that I pinned to my curls and allowed the mesh veil that came attached to it come over my eyes to hide me from the world.

After all this time I couldn't believe that I was back in Rochester, New York. When Chloe kidnapped Mye and pawned him off to Ms. Louise, I swore I'd never return to this city again. There had been just too many bad memories here. There were turning out to be too many bad memories everywhere I went. I vowed to put the past behind me once and for all, but here I was. At the funeral of a man I had only heard about, the only cousin of my husband.

Trying my best to hide behind my veil, I heard sniffles. Snot being inhaled to the back of a throat. Lots of it. Just the mere sound of sadness made my heart sink, and the hairs on my arm stood up. I looked around at the people who came to say their last goodbyes and saw watery eyes, but there were tears in most cases streaming down faces.

Before we got here, I contemplated asking Brooklyn to let me and the kids just stay in our hotel room. We were staying at The Radisson downtown, and I just wanted to rest, but decided against asking him. With me acting crazy in the last couple of days, I knew that I had lost his trust. My husband felt safer with all of us together. Where he could keep his eyes on us. On me.

The church was packed.

Tuff was not from the Roc, but was bred out of Brooklyn, and also had just got out of prison, which to me, slimmed his chances of actually knowing all of these people. I found that quite unusual, until I remembered that the people that died in Rochester became stars, if only for a moment, and were just as quickly forgotten soon after.

Weird, I thought to myself, as I watched the mourners view the body for the last time. A whiff of death in the disguise of roses breezed past my nose as I inhaled the forest of red flowers that rested alongside his pearl black coffin.

I coughed.

Gagged.

"Oshyn, are you okay?" Brooklyn asked, as he quickly started patting my back. I was fine. Just became slightly dizzy and a little nauseous as I recalled having to put that rose on Micah's coffin.

And on Apple's.

And on my grandmother's.

I coughed and gagged again. And again.

"Give me the baby," Brooklyn insisted, as he tried prying him from my arms.

"No! No! Get off of him!" I screamed.

In my outside voice again.

I snatched my son back, away from his father's arms like we were children fighting over a basketball, because I had turned into a mother, fighting over her sanity. I watched the crowd turn their attention from the dead body to watch me. Didn't realize that I was that loud.

"Baby, he can't breathe," Brooklyn said.

Rocking myself back and forth, I looked down and realized that I was holding Mye so tight that his nose was pressing against my chest. My baby *couldn't* breathe. I turned to look at Bella, who still had her earphones glued to her ears, rolling her eyes at me in disgust. Sick of my shenanigans, sick of my bi-polar tendencies.

"Let me hold him for just a little bit," Brooklyn asked, trying not to make more of a scene that I already caused.

I shook my head no. Just couldn't fathom the idea of my baby not being in my arms. Risking the idea of losing him forever. Nobody could protect him like I could, so I needed to make sure that he stayed in the place where he was safest at.

My arms.

Brooklyn left the situation alone, and the crowd went back to handling their business. After everyone had their turn, the pallbearers closed the casket. The Pastor of the church asked the congregation to rise while he prayed. Everyone obeyed his command except for me. While they stood to their feet, I continued to sit.

Fighting with myself.

Because of the war going on in my mind.

Begging my mind not to flash back to the day when eight pallbearers in dark suits carried two coffins in and out of the church I once loved. The day where the sky cried the tears my eyes could no longer produce. The day Brooklyn stood in the distance and I thought I'd never see him again. Losing the battle, my mind went back to the moment I tried to pick Micah up out of his casket with the wish to just hug my baby boy one more time.

But his body was stiff.

Cold.

His once soft skin that always smelled like baby lotion now felt like leather and carried a scent of rosemary. His mouth that kept me laughing had now been glued together, permanently shutting him up forever.

My baby was not my baby.

His soul was no longer there.

Bella's persistent taps on my shoulder broke me out of my daze, and although we weren't on good terms, and it was incredibly annoying, I was grateful. I was heading down-ward fast and she brought me back to reality.

"What?" I whispered to her, wondering how long it had been since everyone took their seats.

"I have to go pee!" she shot back, as usual with a major attitude. She must've been holding it in for a while, be-cause she began squirming in her seat.

"Didn't I tell your little ass to pee before this shit got started?" I waited for a response that I didn't really want. "You're really working my nerves," I told her through my teeth. "Brooklyn, I'll be right back. I'm going to take Bella to the bathroom really quick."

He looked at me for a moment without saying a word, and finally just shook his head from side to side.

"No, I'll take her. You just stay here with him," he demanded, pointing to Mye.

"But you have to read the eulogy," I reminded him. "That has to be coming up anytime now."

"It doesn't matter, I'll take her," he insisted, as he motioned for her to get up. "And don't you fuckin' move!" he threatened me, just as I had done Bella seconds before.

They got up and left, heading toward the entrance of the building. My husband had officially turned into my father, which would explain his recent actions. Like why he talked to me the way he did, and why he hadn't touched me in a while.

Since my birthday.

One week ago.

A week of not having sex to most people is normal, but it wasn't for us. Since the day me and him reunited and recommitted our vows to one another, we made love daily no matter what. His desires for me were so strong that he wouldn't even let my period detour him from *his* pussy. But lately, since my outbursts, he refused to look at me with the lustful gray eyes I'd become accustomed to. No longer did he spoon me at night, and the sweet nothings he used to whisper in my ears had been replaced with silence. I was no longer the woman he married, but a mere stranger he wished he could get a divorce from.

Missing everything the Pastor just said because of my daydreaming, I was at least able to catch him handing the microphone over to a fat lady wearing a purple dress and sporting a big brown Chaka Khan wig. She didn't introduce herself. Never said anything about the deceased. Just belted out a powerful melody of Jesus' healing power.

Those fat people sure know how to sing, I thought to myself, wondering if there was some kind of science that

105

proved that theory. Her voice sent chills up my spine, and at the same time startled Mye as he began to whine. I turned around and looked back to see if I saw any signs of Brooklyn and Bella. *I knew I should've taken her myself*, I thought, as I wondered what was taking them so long. I turned my attention back to Barney, trying to enjoy the rest of the song while Mye continued to squirm in my hands.

"Shhh, it's okay, Mommy is here," I assured him. My attempt to pacify him was of no help, and suddenly I caught a whiff of the culprit.

A shitty diaper.

I looked behind me again, hoping to see the two of them returning, but all I saw were the mourners. Trying to be a wife that obeyed her husband, I decided to stay put in my seat instead of going to the bathroom and changing him, but Mye's squirms got more and more intense, and his cries grew louder than just within my hearing range. *I'm going to look back one more time, and if they are not there, I'm just going to go*, I negotiated with myself. *He'll understand*, I told myself, as I peeked over my shoulder one more time.

And I saw her.

Again.

My eyes grew wider as I gasped for air. "Chloe's here," I said out loud, by mistake. Even though I could only see the lower half of her face because of the oversized black Kentucky Derby hat that was used to cover it, she didn't fool me. I could tell my sister from anywhere.

"Oh!" I screamed, clutching my heart with the hand I had free. "You just scared the shit out of me!" I told Brooklyn, wondering why they didn't come back the same way they left. He looked at me and rolled his eyes like a bitch.

I wanted to tell him.

Wanted him to see what I saw. There was no way that he could've missed it this time. He had to know that Chloe was in the same building that we were in. I turned around and planted my eyes in the same spot I initially saw her in, and realized that she was nowhere to be found. I imitated the exorcist, as my head uncontrollably whirled around in an attempt to find her.

"What in the hell is wrong with you now?" Brooklyn yelled, not realizing that everyone in the church had paused to watch all the excitement in the second row.

"Like I told you in the bathroom," Bella said, directing her comment to Brooklyn, "she's crazy!"

Too wired up to pimp slap her, I ignored Bella's comments. I had bigger issues to deal with, and this brat was going to have to wait. I turned my attention back to Brooklyn and parted my lips to say something, but nothing came out. My intuition was warning me not to tell him what I saw, but I had to. I grabbed his hand, and with tears streaming down my face said, "Chloe's here."

"Get the fuck off of me, Oshyn," he said angrily, as he snatched his hand out of mine. "Seriously? You're going to do this here? At my cousin's funeral?"

"And now I'd like to call up Brooklyn Jones to read the eulogy," the Pastor butted in, sensing that something inappropriate was about to go down.

Without thinking twice, my husband took the first opportunity to get away from me. While he walked into the pulpit, I glanced over my shoulders once more to see if I could get just one more look at her, but there was nothing. Brooklyn stood before the audience looking handsome as ever and began his monologue.

"Ummm," he said nervously, as he stopped to scratch his head. "He was the only cousin I had. He was funny, charming, and always wanted to be like me when he grew up," he said, in an attempt of humor. It failed. "He..."

He stopped because of what he saw. What I had been trying to get him to see for the longest. Within a blink of an eye, Chloe came out of nowhere and was now standing directly in front of the casket, waving at him. He looked at me, and he didn't have to say a word because his eyes said it all.

He was sorry.

"Is that Chloe?" Bella asked with a trembling voice. I

107

shook my head yes, right before I dumped Mye into her lap, got out of my seat and headed to my sister as fast as my black patent leather Louboutins pumps would allow. Chloe turned around and faced me as soon as I reached her.

"Well hello, Oshyn. It's so glad to see you again," she said sarcastically.

I couldn't believe my eyes. I was face to face with a woman who killed my whole family. A woman who was supposed to be dead herself, but here she was in front of me, in front of my husband, alive and well.

I balled up my fist before she was able to get the next sentence out, and punched her dead in the mouth, so hard that she had to catch her fall onto the casket. I followed it up with several more body blows that she wasn't able to come back from, and before the people got around to stopping me, I kicked her in the stomach.

Her fumble made the casket rock.

And then I kicked her again.

And again.

And again.

Until she fell on the floor. Sadly, seconds later the casket followed, causing Tuff's body to lie next to hers. Just as I was about to go in on her further, I received a punch in my stomach that knocked me to my knees. I looked around to see where the fist had come from, as I knew Chloe wasn't the culprit. For starters, she was sprawled out on the floor, and the punch I received couldn't have come from a woman. All of a sudden I noticed that Brooklyn had a man pinned up under his body while he beat the shit out of him furiously. One punch after another, he pounded the tall, slender Michael Jordan look alike.

The guy that I saw sitting next to Chloe.

That bastard must've come to her defense and punched me off of her, I thought, wondering how everything happened so fast. I was able to get a quick glimpse over at my children, who were still seated where I had left them. Bella and the rest of the audience had their eyes glued on us, not wanting to miss one piece of the action.

While Brooklyn continued to bash the strange dude's head in, I made my way back over to Chloe, who no longer had her hat on, exposing what her evil lifestyle had done to her once beautifully flawless appearance. Burn marks and scars were now permanent fixtures in her life. While she was getting dudes for money, I remember trying to warn her that her beauty would fade.

I always knew that she would learn.

The hard way.

By the time I reached Chloe, she had gained some strength and began swinging on me, doing a power punch drill. And just as I was about to swing back, I heard a shot.

One bullet.

A loud one…piercing to the ears.

Stopped us in our tracks.

Stopped everyone in their tracks.

I quickly turned to see if the kids were okay, but before my eyes made it to them I saw Brooklyn fall to his knees in slow motion. Blood spilled out of him as I ran over to him and placed my hands over his, trying my best to keep it in, but I couldn't figure out where it was coming from.

"I love you," was the only thing he said as the color began to escape from his pigment.

"No, baby, please don't do this to me. Don't go!" I screamed, but my cries fell on deaf ears as I watched his eyes close and his breaths come to a screeching halt. "No! No! No! No! Come on, baby, open your eyes. Don't go to sleep…stay with me!" I felt his soul leave his body, as everyone around me reacted frantically.

A female bystander ran to my side and placed her index and middle finger on his neck. Before I knew it her once hopeful eyes turned to sadness. "He's gone," she confirmed.

Chloe and the man that had murdered my husband were nowhere to be found, and I knew that the police were on their way. All of me wanted to stay by his side and just hold him in my arms. I just wanted to be able to tell the police what happened, and be assured that they would handle that bitch once and for all, but I knew that couldn't happen. Couldn't risk them taking me into custody or separating me and the kids.

If I could take his dead and lifeless body with me, I would, but that was impossible. Before I could put too much more thought into it, I got up drenched in blood and ran to Bella. Without having to tell her anything, she grabbed up all Mye's stuff and ran out the church with me, as we left the man of our home on the floor next to his cousin.

May they both rest in peace.

Chapter Fifteen
(Chloe)

"I don't have any beef!" Carlos said angrily, as he swerved his rental car in and out of traffic, trying to get as far away from the murder scene as he could. "I just shot a man…killed him and it wasn't *my* beef!"

He seemed disturbed by the fact that he had rescued me, but that was something that he would get over. I was floating on cloud nine at the image of him and Brooklyn fighting over me. Over my love. They were the two men that the gypsy predicted. *That bitch did know what she was talking about*, I thought, as I finally began to feel like I was in heaven again.

"I didn't even want to go to that funeral!" he continued to complain, and he was right. Although we had spent the last two days together, I had to remember that he didn't have to stay with me past all the free pussy I was throwing at him. But there was something about our union that seemed unbreakable. That seemed real. That seemed predestined.

From the beginning he didn't want to go to the funeral. Rochester wasn't his hometown, and he was only in town to promote another huge event. A Live Nation concert with Jay Z. A concert that would bring in well over six figures.

He had every right to be mad.

Me and my problems were fucking with his money, but he was a true gentleman for accompanying me, insisting that he didn't want me to go and mourn alone. Especially since I told him who Tuff was to me.

My ex-boyfriend.

With whom I broke up with because he started to date my cousin.

I chuckled to myself at the shit I came up with. A lesson I never forgot when it came to dealing with these niggas was that all of them loved a woman that was taken. It heightened my stock. Anything involving another man was better than saying you were single. It screams desperate and that was far from what I was.

"What in the hell was that all about anyway?" he asked, expecting a legit reason of why he just smoked a dude in broad daylight. One he didn't even know.

"I just wanted to see him one more time before he was buried, but she was there. Oshyn, the one that stole him from me," I lied, trying to drum up some tears from a well that ran dry. "I didn't want to cause a scene, so I went up while everybody was quiet, thinking that she wouldn't say anything in a crowd of mourners, but that bitch never had any respect for anyone else other than herself."

I spoke with my head held down, trying to seem sad about something, trying to disguise the happiness in my voice that revealed how pleased I was that Brooklyn was out of the picture. Because if I couldn't have him, nobody would. But Carlos said nothing. There was extreme silence in the car. Only one of his hands was on the steering wheel, so I grabbed the right one that lay on his thigh and whispered, "Thank you."

I was in love.

This was finally my destiny.

Before my dreams of answered prayers could go any further into a future for us, I noticed a black Yukon with blacked out tinted windows following us. The truck towered over us compared to the SL 550 Benz that Carlos rented

112

from the luxury car rental spot. With one monster truck
move, we'd be smashed like a can of sardines. Not wanting
to involve him in anymore avoidable drama, I decided not to
mention the stalker.

I wasn't sure when the truck started tailing us, but we
had only been driving for ten minutes, and I noticed them following us for at least five of them. We came to a split in the
expressway and he took 390-North, going toward Buffalo,
New York instead of 390-South, which was in the direction of
our hotel.

"You don't have to run," I let him know just in case he
was planning his escape route. "This is Rochester. No one
snitches, period."

"I'm not worried about that," he advised me, looking
out of his rearview mirror. "Do you know who this truck is following us?"

I looked behind me as if I hadn't seen them all along
and shook my head no. The entire car was pitch black. Even
the front windshield was way too dark to see through. *Nah, it
couldn't be*, I thought, trying to shut out the idea that it
could've been Oshyn. *That bitch doesn't have the balls*, I
concluded. But the thought of it actually being her wouldn't
go away. My man had just killed her husband, so I was sure
that the pair of balls she never had she'd quickly grown into.

Suddenly, the truck ran up on us, hitting the back end
of our car. *Where are the fucking police when you need
them?* I asked myself sarcastically, knowing that I didn't want
to see those bastards. I was glad we had our seatbelts on,
as we jolted forward when the truck hit us again, this time
breaking one of the tail lights.

"Who in the hell is that?" Carlos asked, as he struggled to keep control of the car.

I stayed silent, not really able to come up with any
real answers as to who or what was going on. Finally tired of
playing with us, the truck hit the gas and pulled along my
side of the car, making sure to keep up with our speed.

The window of the truck cracked open. Not far

enough to actually see her face, just to let us know that there was an actual human in the car. And then I saw the barrel of the gun slide through the small opening.

"Oh shit, Oshyn found us!" I screamed as I bent down, attempting to get as low to the floor as I could. I knew that the kids were with her, because that bitch wouldn't let them out of her sight, especially with me back in the picture. But I couldn't believe that she would put them in harm's way. She had finally lost her fucking mind. Like I had long ago.

Carlos slightly lost control of the car when he looked over and saw the reason for my sudden panic, and before the both of us could react, the trigger had been pulled.

The gun fired.

Knowing that it was Oshyn had now been confirmed. I could tell by the way that she missed the car. No professional would've missed a mark that was so close. That bitch was never gangsta. Just pretended to be. And then my phone rang.

Probably Tommy, I assumed while ignoring it, but it rang over and over and over again. Something that old man would dare not do. I finally picked it up.

"What!" I asked agitated. I had just avoided gunshots aimed at me, and was in absolutely no mood for playing on the phone. The caller hung up, and I knew that it was definitely not Tommy as the hospital number would have come up on my called ID, but this number came up private. It rang again, and this time I answered it on the first ring.

"Hello?"

No answer.

I put the ringer on silent and threw it down on the floor. There were bigger things for me to worry about, like dodging bullets from the woman that wanted me dead the most. We were already going ninety miles per hour on this expressway, as the Yukon hit the gas and sped past us, jumping in front of our car.

Carlos slammed on his breaks as his car had no choice but to hit hers, damaging the front end of his rental

114

severely, and ending with us up in a ditch. Oshyn pulled over to the median, stopping a few feet ahead of us.

"Do you have your gun on you?" I asked, after realizing that I had no protection on me.

"No, I got rid of that shit. It was evidence," Carlos remarked.

I quickly began to panic as I watched the driver side door swing open, and a pair of legs popped out and touched the ground. With the gun in her hand, and long luxurious curly hair flowing from her scalp, I realized that this wasn't Oshyn at all.

"What the fuck?" I said aloud, wondering who this random chick could be. She was absolutely beautiful and thick in all the right places. Like I used to be. And she was definitely my type. Sexy and deadly, but I couldn't figure out who her beef was with. I knew Carlos wasn't from here, but he threw enough major concerts in this town to learn how to get around as well as he did and to grab a few chicken heads here and there.

"Nina?" he blurted out, as she inched closer.

Not sure how he was able to see anything past the barrel of the gun that she had aimed at his head, but men were stupid. All men were stupid.

"Who is she?" I asked, as she walked up to his side of the car, but I got no answer. A few cars whisked past us, going way too fast to notice the danger we were in. With no protection to save us, we were on our own.

"Who is she?" the girl asked, pointing the gun at me. "Is she the reason you don't come home anymore?"

"Nina, are you fucking crazy? How did you find me?" Carlos asked, with an obvious hint of confusion in his voice.

"I tapped your phone. Sprint Family Locator. Only five dollars additional each month. Tells me everything. Where you are, where you just came from, how long you stayed, what route you took to get there. Everything."

"So, you drove all the way here from the city? That's five hours?" he said confused.

She stared at him, not really seeming to want to answer the question, but did anyway.

"I knew I couldn't get you in Saint Tropez, and you stopped answering my calls so I came to you." She paused again. Then looked at me. "So, this broke busted bitch is the reason?"

"Fuck you," I blurted out. I knew I was taking a chance talking shit with no weapon, but I couldn't just let her talk to me like that. It would have ruined my reputation.

"What did you say?" she asked, as she took the gun back off of Carlos and pointed it back in my direction.

"I said fuck...."

The gun went off again.

This bitch is crazy, I said laughing to myself, as I tried to figure out where the bullet had gone. I definitely wasn't hit.

She couldn't shoot for shit, but she was certifiably crazy. I found her amusing. Not a threat anymore, but more like entertainment. If she wanted to shoot us, she would've done it by now, but by her reckless actions, she wasn't a true gangsta like me. She played too much. Liked the attention. She was a pussy. Smelled her from a mile away.

"Say one more thing and I'm going to blow your fucking brains out!" she warned.

"Yeah, a'ight," I said sarcastically.

"What?"

"Man, talk to your nigga. I don't have shit to do with your situation," I roared."

Tired of watching us talk back and forth, Carlos took control of the situation by getting out of the car. Guess he sensed her seriousness about actually shooting someone also, as he no longer seemed afraid to take action.

"Where is my son at?" he asked her.

"Son? You don't have a son anymore, bastard! Make one with this bitch. My son is with his new fath..."

Before the last part of her words could be formed, Carlo took Nina's long locks, entangled them tightly in his fingers, and smashed her head into the hood of the wrecked

Benz. When he lifted her head back up it was filled with blood, and before I got a chance to see what other damage had been done, he took her head and rammed it through the glass windshield, cracking it. She lifted her head with her mouth open, and I noticed this time teeth were missing.

"Don't you ever talk like that about my son again, you stupid bitch!" he warned. After knocking her teeth out, he threw her on the ground and stomped her out. She lay motionless as his thrusts got more aggressive. When he finally came to a stop, he ordered me out the car.

"For what?" I asked him confused. "You're not going to beat the shit out of me!"

"Man, get out! We're can't drive in this car anymore. We're going to get in the truck." *So much for this rental*, I thought, as I noticed all the irreparable damage that had been done. I opened the door and got out, making my way to the other car.

"What about the rental? Can this be traced back to you?"

"Come on, baby, don't let my image fool you. I'm a street dude. Nothing can be traced back to me." We both got in the truck and drove away. Together at last.

Me, Bonnie.

Him, Clyde.

Chapter Sixteen
(Oshyn)

I lay curled up in a fetal position in the corner of my hotel room. Mye cried hysterically, while Bella did all she could to calm him down, but to no avail. He wanted his mother's love and his father's touch, but neither was at his disposal. Brooklyn's touch had been torn from our grasp forever, while my heart had been ripped to shreds.

Irreparable.

Like shattered glass.

At least an hour had floated by since we rushed out of the funeral, leaving Brooklyn all alone at his own murder scene. The same place he went to bid farewell to someone else's life, was the same place his very own had come to a cruel ending. I continued to rock my pain away, as Mye reached for me. Unable to be the mother he needed me to be, Bella took control by picking him up off the bed. She walked him around the room, trying as best as she could to soothe him, something I knew she needed herself.

Because we were all hurting.

My baby's cries grew quieter and quieter as I smothered my tears into the last t-shirt my husband had on before we left earlier that day. I inhaled his sweet sweaty scent and instantly began to cry.

"My last words to him weren't I love you!" I screamed, startling Mye again into the same sea of tears that Bella took so long to stop.

Normally she would've said something smart by now, but death had taken its toll on her as well. By the way she looked at me, she knew that I needed her help, so she walked over to me with my baby in her hands and sat down beside me.

She didn't say anything. Just sat there speechless while I lost my mind. She even attempted to stroke my hair that had become out of control, but nothing helped. I was now a widower to the man I was supposed to grow old with. To the man who stole my heart the very first time I laid my eyes on him. To the man who asked me to be his wife.

I remember the first time I saw him at church two years ago in North Carolina. I couldn't keep my eyes off of him, and then we officially met at the bookstore later that day. I recalled giving him such a hard time when he tried to pay for my books, but all he was trying to be was a gentle-man. Just didn't want to admit to myself that I could actually love again, especially after all the drama I had gone through with Micah's dad, Trent.

My mind went back to the night I placed my hand in his and stared into his light gray eyes, saying yes when asked to be his wife. It was like destiny refused for me and Brooklyn to be apart. Even the heartache of catching him in the bed with Chloe while we were on our honeymoon wasn't strong enough to separate us. Because he was my Adam and I was his Eve. Our souls had been mended together, and the little piece of life I had left had died with him.

I had become the living dead.

Then out of nowhere, Bella snapped me out of my dreams with her cries. Millions of tears stormed out of her eyes, as she showed how physically upset she was. And then she spit it out. Big brown chunks of what she had to eat for the day now laid next to us as we did the best we could to handle the situation. Couldn't believe that we weren't used to this by now, because we weren't amateurs at mourning death. As her crying outburst simmered down, I heard a knock at the door.

"Be quiet," I whispered to her, in an attempt to calm her whimpering down. 'Shhhh, somebody is knocking on the door."

She wiped a few tears away from her face, and stared at the same door that my eyes had become glued to.

"I didn't hear anything," she said confused. I caught her looking at me from my side view as she continued. "Did you hear me, I don't think anyone is at the…"

"Shhhh," I repeated. "I heard it again." I stood to my feet, not knowing what my next move would be. "Maybe its Brooklyn," I said, with a hint of excitement in my voice. I managed to crack a grin at even just the thought of seeing the small gap that accompanied his smiles.

Not being able to bare the thought of it being my husband on the other side of the door, I ran to it and unlatched the locks that kept us away from each other. I opened the door with expectancy in my heart, not being able to contain the feeling of him in my arms one more time.

"Brooklyn?" I said as I turned my head from side to side, staring down the hotel hallway. "Brooklyn, where are you?"

"It's not him," I heard a woman's voice say, and then I saw her. She was just as beautiful as the last time I lay my eyes on her.

"Mama?"

"Jes, its jur grandmother and I come to help ju." I let her in and closed the door behind us, noticing that her Puerto Rican accent was as strong as before. "Oh my goodness," she continued, as she placed her old, wrinkly hands over her mouth. "Jus look at Bella. She is so big and muy bonita. And the baby es muy grande. Oh, I just wish Micah could see this!"

"I missed you so much, Mama. How is Micah and Apple's doing?"

"Oh, don't ju worry about them, they are both doing fine," she assured me.

I wanted to bombard her with questions regarding them, but she didn't seem like she came to talk about it.

"Auntie, what's going on?" Bella asked, with a terrified look on her face. "Who are you talking to?"

"Don't you see her? It's Mama...my grandmother. Don't you remember her?" I asked, as I pointed in her direction.

"But...but...nobody is there," Bella responded slowly. Her body seemed to tense up, and her voice trembled as she continued. "Why are you talking to yourself?"

"Don't be rude!" I shot back at her. 'You *will* respect her!" I turned back to my grandmother, who had taken a seat on the bed, and apologized for Bella's smart mouth. "I just don't know what has gotten into her lately," I confessed, as I sat down beside her.

"It's okay, baby. Ju are jus stressed from what happened today. But I came to tell ju that everything is going to be jus fine." And before she got another word out, I broke down.

"She was supposed to be dead, but she managed to take him from me!"

"You're scaring me," Bella said, interrupting me. "What's going on?"

"Don't you see me speaking to a grown up?"

"Shhh, calm down, sweetheart. She's jus scared too, ju know? Been through a lot herself, but don't get angry with her. Be patient and she'll grow up to be a good woman." I missed her wisdom and her meek spirit dearly, as she calmed me down instantly. "Ju know what ju have to do?"

"What?" I asked, thinking that she was still referring to Bella.

"Ju have to get rid of her once and for all. Kill Chloe. That's the only way."

Kill Chloe, I thought to myself, as I wondered what would make her say that to me. That was out of her character. Something that she would have never recommended to me on any other day, but maybe there was something she knew that I didn't.

"That child is evil and must be put down, but ju are the only one that can do it. If ju don't, she will murder ju and the rest of jur children. A slow and painful death. This is jur warning."

"But how am I going to do that? I can't take them with me. That'll be leaving them in too much danger, and I don't have anyone I can trust them with."

"Ju go and I will watch over them. Everything will be okay, I promise."

I looked at Bella, who was sobbing silently in the corner, and then took a quick glance at Mye, who was sound asleep in her arms. I walked over to her and kneeled down to talk to her.

"I have to go now," I told her. "I have to take care of Chloe before she comes back to hurt you guys."

"No, please don't leave us here," Bella pleaded with me, visibly scared out of her mind.

"No, everything is going to be okay," I promised, as I kissed her forehead. "I need you to be strong now. Take care of Mye for me, and I'll be back to get the both of you tomorrow."

"But I can't take care of a baby…I'm only nine," she revealed, as if I didn't know.

"You'll do fine. Just order room service for your food, and fix Mye those bottles," I said, pointing to the refrigerator. "I'll be back before you run out. And my grandmother will be here too. Don't worry, you won't be alone."

"Please don't leave me here with a ghost. You were talking to a dead person! Please don't go…I'm so scared." Snot now fell as freely out of her nose as the tears followed.

"Oshyn, it's time. Ju have to go now," Mama said, hinting at me to say my goodbyes. I kissed Bella again, and planted my lips on my son, praying that I would see them both again. But this was something I knew I had to do if we

123

were going to live a long life. I walked toward the door, and when I reached it, I grabbed onto the handle, looking back one more time at my family.

"Kill her," was the last thing I heard as I walked out, not having a clue what I was getting ready to get myself into.

Chapter Seventeen
(Oshyn)

9:30 a.m.

IHop parking lot.

It's where I had slept.

It was a brand new day, and I still found myself on the hunt for Chloe. The four hours of sleep had done some good, but my mental state still needed work.

The violent toss and turns I endured, while trying to get some rest, pretty much kept me up the entire night. The nightmare that I wished was a dream had come true, and now haunted me in my attempts to get some sleep. No matter how hard I tried, I couldn't get Brooklyn out of my mind. Couldn't get the fact that he had died in my arms out of my mind. I couldn't get anything out of my mind.

Even though I was in the hood, I didn't worry about anyone coming to attack me. My life had already been ruined, so if somebody came at me…they would be the one in shock. My knife fit snuggly in my front pocket and was easily accessible. I wasn't the Oshyn everyone thought they knew. I was the new Oshyn. The Oshyn who'd lost her husband. The Oshyn who was now all alone. And the Oshyn who would learn to commit murder.

The sound of the word murder caused my neck to

swivel toward the passenger seat. I had to make sure my two-toned tan sack was still on the floor. Its contents; duct-tape, rope, mace, and acid were all important to me. Crucial to the mission. I leaned forward, spotted the sack then started up the vehicle.

As soon as I adjusted my mirror, I got a wake-up call. My hair was matted and spread all over my head. With my bare hands I patted my head, hoping to do enough to get by. It was bad enough not having a change of clothes, or a wash cloth to clean my face, but my hair needed to lie down to keep me from looking crazy. Couldn't risk any unwanted attention being drawn to me. I needed to get rid of her and get out of this city as fast I could.

When I pulled out the lot, I realized the gas tank was close to empty, so gas was at the top of my list. What else could be expected? I had spent all night looking for Chloe, and had driven around for hours with no luck. I even checked where we used to live.

Nothing.

Not one sign of that bitch.

I wasn't sure why, but I even checked my grand-mother's old neighborhood. It was her suggestion. She coached me, even told me a new way to get there. Her neighbor, Miss Rose, was surprised to see me, but after she told me why, I understood. Chloe had indeed been through the neighborhood, and told Miss Rose that I was dead. No longer on the face of the earth. I told her if she saw Chloe again to call me. I then went on a rampage to find her since I knew she was still in town.

Chloe had no friends that I could turn to for answers. She could never keep even one, not even an associate. Always fucked their men behind their backs, or simply stabbed them in the back. I was in this alone, and wasn't looking forward to the mission. It was almost 10 a.m. with no new clues, and I had become incredibly frustrated. A hint of emotion took over.

Within seconds, I pulled over, put the car in park, and

126

burst into tears. In that quick instance, images of my husband flooded my mind. I cried out like a baby, wishing he were with me. I thought about his sweet touch, his soft lips, and the way he took care of me.

"Whyyyyyyyy Brooklyn! Whyyyyyyy!" I bawled. I banged my head against the wheel and sobbed some more. "I need you, baby. I need you! Do you hear me, Brooklyn?"

I had become enslaved to my emotions, which was why it took more than an hour for me to bounce back. I had to keep sniveling and sniffling up my snot, trying to get myself together. Able to drive within the white lines again. Then my big break came. The phone rang from a Rochester area code. It didn't take long for me to answer and get the 411 on Chloe. My investigative work had paid off, as I told an old classmate, "You saw her where? You sure it was Chloe?"

I questioned hard.

I hung up in a rage and started down highway 390 East then got off on Clinton Avenue, just three exits down. It was a trashy neighborhood, dirty. A place I wasn't feeling at all. A far cry from St. Tropez, it was where crackheads roamed, and all the welfare recipients hung out. As I drove down Clinton, I noticed the going out of business signs that hung high in some windows, and the boarded up spots where the owners had just given up.

I stopped dead in my tracks when I spotted her. She was outside an old factory that had closed down near Hart Street. My mind raced, wondering what she was up to, and how I would make my move. It looked as if she'd just had a meeting with someone in an old Buick. I just wasn't one hundred percent sure.

Before she could make it back to her car, I revved on the gas and picked up speed. I found myself chasing her onto the sidewalk, and she began to run like a bat out of hell. It was like something out of the movie, *Heat*. No holds bar. It amazed me how fast her ass could run, spiked six inch heels and all. She'd never done anything athletic as a child. Guess her life being on the line brought changes.

Quick changes.

I was sure I looked crazy the way I gripped the wheel with both hands and leaned as far into it as I could go. But fortunately the lot was mostly bare, with the exception of a few bystanders, who either held brown paper bags containing liquor, or were looking for their next hit.

I heard someone yell out, "Look at her!" They pointed at me, then attempted to point at Chloe, until she made it to the end of the deserted strip mall, and darted around the back.

Like a mad woman, I followed her and swerved the car off the sidewalk onto the pavement and turned on two wheels toward the back. Wherever Chloe had gone, I was sure she was out of breath. It didn't matter where she had run off and hid, or what kind of gun she had, because I wasn't going to back down. Not this time. I kept my grip tight, while rotating my neck from side to side, trying to sniff out any kind of movement. That's when I saw it. The long, denim part of her shirt.

She moved like a snake behind a big, blue trash can nestled behind the factory warehouse door. I revved on the gas again, picked up speed, and in no time stopped abruptly in front of the closing door. I'm sure she thought she had escaped. That just simply wasn't the case.

I had her.

I knew it.

For the first time, my own blood would die at my hands, I told myself, hopping from the car. I almost forgot my sack, until I doubled back, grabbed it and made the door to the alarm chirp. I didn't care if Chloe knew I was coming in. Because I wanted her to know that her time here on earth was coming to an end.

Inside, things felt eerie. There was a damp feeling, and the smell of mildew accompanied it. I took baby steps, while searching for a light switch, all along watching my back. The darkness had me spooked, plus the fact that Chloe was a slick bitch. I kept doing police moves, stopping

128

at every corner before I moved further.

Then I saw her.

Standing three yards away from me.

We faced each other like two boxers headed to our corners of the ring. It was weird, because all sort of emotions flooded my body. To me, she was beautiful. She was family. But today, I would keep our family tradition alive. She would die at the hands of me, and be buried before her time. But truth be told, she was my cousin, my sister, one of my few remaining living relatives.

"Oshyn. My dear Oshyn," Chloe called out to me. Her heels clicked on the hard floor and she grinned wickedly. "So good to see you," she said, with disdain in her voice. "This is good," she nodded, and paced the floor like it was a good thing we were now in the same room.

I walked toward her, making sure I kept my confidence up. I had thrown my bag over my shoulder, and kept my right hand near the front pocket of my jeans. I couldn't help but wonder if she too had a weapon. Oddly enough, she kept her fingers at her side.

"We need to talk, Chloe. I mean we're family."

I made a funny movement with my cheeks, then purred like a harmless kitten.

She snarled. "Most of your family is dead, bitch. They just waiting on you." She laughed wildly.

Out of the blue, I dug into my pocket, flipped open my blade, and let a victory grin seep through the sides of my lips. As I held the knife in her direction her facial expression changed.

"Look here cuz, sis, or whatever you want to call me. Let me put your dumb ass onto something. I think you really need to know some good news since Brooklyn's dead."

Damn, it was about my late husband. And it was good? Maybe I did need to know, I told myself, getting choked up again.

"Why, Chloe? Why did it happen?"

She moved closer, and so did I. For once, she was

sincere as she told me the guy she was with at the funeral had tried to kill her too. He was trying to frame her. When she told me that he followed her to the funeral, and made his move on her there, I was shocked. I felt bad for her just as I thought about my honey once again. Chloe could see the sadness in my face as I wept like a baby in front of her. The tough girl role had come to an end momentarily.

I threw my hands across the upper part of my face in an attempt to hide my misery. The blade stuck out from my fingers, but I still had a decent grip. Huge tears began to fade my vision. But it didn't bother my sense of touch. It was Chloe behind me. I could feel her coldness and her sense-less touch. Without warning, she managed to snatch the weapon from my hand and wrap her dominant arm around my neck. Slowly she told me I was still naïve. Still stupid. And now I would be joining Grandma, Apples, Micah and Brooklyn in the depths of hell.

Chloe had tricked me.

I should have known better.

And now I would pay for my stupidity.

She inched me along, still with a good grip on my neck, looking for a place to settle. Finally, she pushed me down onto the only chair in the place. From what I could see it was metal, uneven, and barely enough space to hold my plump ass. It didn't matter, Chloe had the blade clinched deep into the skin of my neck, and refused to allow me the freedom to move. My butt was placed firmly in the seat as she stared at me for minutes confusingly. Suddenly, she snatched the rope from my bag and began to tie me up with her left hand, while still letting the knife hold my neck hostage with her right hand. At first the rope seemed to be loose until she had me in a controlling bundle. Then it became tighter and tighter, as she looped the rope around several more times.

I flinched a little as the rope tightened, yet my soul wouldn't allow me to show any fear. That's what she had been used to all our lives. Assuming that I was scared of

130

anything that didn't look or smell right. And she, the rebel, the gansta bitch who reacted with malice in every situation that came her way. Next, she probed at my feet. She grinned, then went for the duct tape. It was crazy how she'd now used all my tactics against me. Why was I the one sitting in the chair?

My little pep talk about showing no fear meant nothing anymore. The moment I saw Chloe pick up a long, iron piece that had been left on the cold, concrete floor, my heart began thumping at a rapid pace, and tears welled up in my eyes. Everything was happening so fast. Too fast my body warned. But there was nothing more I could do. Chloe beat the rod looking weapon against her forearm as she moved deceitfully my way. Her eyes revealed that she would go all the way. Her smirk told me this was a long time coming.

"C'mon, Chloeeeeeee! Noooooooo! Let's talk about…"

Before I knew it, she'd hit me over the head.

Hard.

Again.

And again.

Until I no longer responded.

Chapter Eighteen
(Oshyn)

"Remember Trent?" Chloe asked me casually, as if we were two girlfriends out on a Sunday brunch. As if we were the reminiscing type. As if he wasn't the father of my firstborn son.

I sat on the steel chair as I slowly regained consciousness, with my hands taped and chained tightly together. The same had been done to my feet, giving me no chance to escape. The blood that had trickled down from my head, now replaced the saliva that was in my mouth. I wasn't quite sure what the damage looked like, but the flow of blood that fell, and the intense throbbing pain I felt let me know that it was serious. Even though I had started to see double, I refused to give up, but at the present moment, my odds of killing Chloe were looking very slim.

"Did you hear me?" Chloe asked me.

I couldn't figure out what she was hinting at about Trent, so I never answered her question. Just sat restlessly in pain, as I tried to calculate what her next move was going to be, so I could be prepared for what was to come next.

She balled up her fist and hit me with two powerful back to back punches in the face, leaving it in excruciating pain, but I never cried. Never even made a sound. Couldn't give her the satisfaction of knowing that she had hurt me anymore than she had.

I just refused to let her take that away from me.

Like she had done everything else in my life.

"Damn it, answer me when I'm fucking talking to you!" she demanded, until she was satisfied that she had gotten my attention. "Now, I'll ask you again...do you remember Trent?"

I nodded my head yes, trying my best to defy her orders. But the next punch she threw landed on my jaw and instantly sent chills down my spine. The blood now poured down my face like a bloody sea, and it was then that I realized that if I had any hope of surviving, I was going to have to play by her rules.

"I have all day," she admitted, as she rubbed the hand that assaulted me. "I've dreamed about this day ever since you left me for dead at that old warehouse, and the day is finally here! And now you're in a warehouse. Seems appropriate, doesn't it?"

I heard the excitement that rose in her voice as she spoke about the torture she had planned for me all this time. The excitement from the thought of my demise. The excitement from the thought of her being responsible for it. Before she got a chance to finish her speech, I broke my silence.

"Yes, I remember Trent. I remember him."

She smiled.

Pleased that I made the choice to give in.

Pleased that she was breaking me down.

Pleased that this was going to be easier than she thought.

"I don't know if our grandmother told you, but I fucked him too. She caught us in her bed...you know, after he put you out. While you were pregnant and in the middle of that snowstorm. Since this is the end of your life, I thought you'd

134

like to be aware of that."

I went back to the day that the man who introduced me to love threw me out of our home and watched through the living room window we once shared, as I went into labor with the bank of snow as my bed. Chloe admitting that she had sex with him wasn't a surprise to me, because I expected nothing better from either of them, so she could've kept her confession to herself. Realizing that her bringing up Trent didn't matter to me, she continued to dig further to gain some kind of reaction from me.

"You stupid bitch, you were never able to keep a man," Chloe revealed, with a smirk on her face. "I fucked them all, but Brooklyn was the best."

She struck a nerve, and my blood instantly began to boil.

"He never loved you!" I blurted out, letting her know that despite how I acted, her words were slowly breaking me down.

At that moment, she laughed a laugh that was so loud that it bounced off the walls. She was cracking herself up at my inability to control myself.

My emotions.

"Oh, trust and believe that he loved me," she said, after catching her breath. "I was having his baby, and it was a pregnancy that was planned. And you killed it. You killed our future, our destiny, our love, and I've returned the favor by killing him. Dead. Like you'll be not too long from now."

And out of nowhere, I started laughing. So hard that it bounced off the same walls Chloe's once did.

"What in the fuck is so funny?" she asked confused.

"You are."

Before I went any further I spit out some blood that had taken over my mouth, and contemplated choosing my words wisely, but decided against it as my fate, at this point, seemed inevitable.

"You always had my sloppy seconds. You may have fucked all my boyfriends, but you had them after me. Step up

135

your game, boo. I know it may be a little harder now that I fucked your face up like that, but maybe after I'm gone and out of the way, you can get a nigga on your own. I won't be a threat anymore, so you don't have to worry about him falling in love with me first."

If I didn't know any better I could've sworn that I saw steam coming out of her nose. I had her hot.

"I have a man," she revealed, in an artless attempt to upstage me in the arena of love.

"Yeah, I'm sure you do."

I rolled my eyes, which was followed by an instant throbbing of my face where it was struck at.

I didn't want her to know that she hurt me, because I knew that there was more to come.

"My man is more successful than Brooklyn ever was. Carlos has more money, a bigger dick, and more balls. As a matter of fact, he proved it by killing your husband…for me."

I noticed a twinkle in her eye as she continued to speak highly of the man who took Brooklyn's life.

"I hope that your children come out retarded, and you die giving birth to those bastards," was all I could think of to say.

She walked over to a small black table and picked up a book of matches. She then lit one and sat the tip of the burning flame on the corner of my eye.

"Awwwww!" were the words that replaced the smart comments, as I felt my skin melting off. She threw the old match on the floor and took another one out, swiping that against the box.

"No…no…no!" was all I could muster up, as she sat the flame on my lip. All I heard was a sizzling sound, as it felt like my skin was being fried.

"How does it feel to be burned?" she asked, pointing to her own third degree wounds on her face.

I didn't answer. Knew it was a trick question. Knew that there was no right or wrong answer. I knew that anything I said would lead to my doom.

136

Noticing that my cooperation was out of the question, she walked back over to the table and picked up a jar that looked to carry two cockroaches in it. She slowly unscrewed the top as they ran around at lightning speed at just the thought of being free once again. She picked one up and brought it over to me, holding it close to my face.

Its long antennas and legs wiggled around, as its big brown body followed suit, trying to get its capturer to let go, but Chloe held on tighter. I tried my best to move my face out of the way as she inched it closer and closer to my face.

"What are you doing?" I asked, struggling to get my hands free.

She remained silent as she aimed the roach toward my ear. I violently yanked my head back and forth, trying my best to get her away, but nothing seemed to work.

Tired of my fighting, Chloe put me in a headlock and stuffed the roach in my ear, and all of the fighting I did proved to be useless as it seemed to make its way into my eardrum.

"Ahhhhh!" I screamed, as the crippling pain of the insect burrowing too far in my ear became unbearable. Excruciating torture were the only words I could use to describe the feelings I had, as I listened to the roach make a home inside of my head.

"Get it out of me!" I yelled, while the movement of its crunchy body echoed in my ear.

"Guess what I found out about roaches?" she asked, as if we were in a class. "I learned that they can go like a week or two without water. Those bastards can even go for several hours without air."

Satisfied that the first roach was lodged into my ear deep enough, she went back to the jar to retrieve the second one from the glass prison it had somehow found its way back into. I began to bang my head as hard as I could against my shoulder, as I felt the disgusting creature tunneling into my brain.

"When I get out of here, I'm going to kill you, bitch!"

was all I could say, as she inserted the other roach into the ear that was free. She stayed put for a little bit, making sure that it had dug itself deep into my canal, and then she walked away.

Although I wondered where she went, I was more concerned with relieving myself of this pain, when she appeared again out of nowhere with a bucket full of water.

"I'm done playing with you. Let's just get this over with. Tell me where the kids are."

Even with all the racket going on in my brain, I heard every word she said, but chose to ignore her as my head did the dance of one who was possessed. Letting me know that she meant business, Chloe took my head and slammed it into the bucket of water, and held it down while I tried my hardest to get up. It was probably a few seconds, but it felt like eternity before she let my head back up for some air.

I gasped for as much air as my lungs would allow, but with the roaches still running rampid in my mind, I began to panic, losing all the extra air that I had left.

"Where are Bella and Mye?" she asked again, with a dead serious face that warned me against trying her.

She was officially done playing with me, and was getting ready to prove it. Even though I wasn't ready to die, I still wasn't able to give my children up for the sake of my freedom.

"Go and kill yourself," was the last thing I said, before she plunged my head back into the water.

My hair floated around carelessly as I held my breath, trying to get a hold of whatever air I could. And then I panicked again after realizing that the luxury of air had no longer been afforded to me. I began to rapidly move my body in an attempt to free myself, but my movements only got me more excited. I fought it for as long as I could, as my breathing reflexes slowly came back.

And I inhaled.

While my head was still submerged under water.

Before I took another breath, Chloe pulled my head

out as I coughed and gagged violently. Trying my best to survive. And then her phone rang.

"Damn it," she said to herself, after taking the phone out of her pocket and reading the name on her caller ID. "I forgot that I was supposed to meet up with Carlos for dinner later on." After talking to herself, she finally decided to answer the phone. "Hey, baby, sorry I…"

She paused.

Then said, "Who is this…Nina?" I watched her reaction closely as she paused again, assuming to let whoever this Nina chick was to talk. "Can I meet you? Ummm, yeah when? Now? Okay, give me a few minutes and I'll meet you at Marketplace Mall."

Chloe asked me once more where the children were, and after I refused to tell, she dumped my head back in the bucket, and kept it in there until this time I lost consciousness.

Chapter Nineteen
(Chloe)

I pulled into the parking lot of Marketplace Mall about twenty minutes after I hung up the phone with Nina. It had only been a couple of days since I watched my man put her head through the windshield of his rental car, and I was curious to see what she looked like. Still very confused about what she was doing with Carlos' phone, my mind was running a million miles per second, trying to drum up the answers. But I was finally here, and I was sure that she would tell me everything I needed to know.

It was her idea to meet here at the mall, which let me know that this wasn't her first trip to Rochester. I walked into the mall, took a seat at one of the tables in the food court, and glanced at my watch.

"This bitch needs to hurry up!" I said out loud, wondering what was taking her so long. I had to get back to Oshyn so that I could get rid of her once and for all.

I looked around, and realized that nothing ever changed in this city, and certainly not in the old ass mall. It had been over two years since I had actually stepped foot in this place, and everything still looked exactly the same. The stores looked the same, and the people all still looked the same. I remembered the trips that my mother would take me on as a little girl to the mall and how excited I was to just be with her.

And now resentment had taken its place because my childhood memories of her were slowly fading away, and this was one of the only places I could recall spending time with her. However, before my mind wandered any further into the excruciating pain of missing her, I noticed Nina sitting at a table not too far from mine.

Watching me.

Closely.

Damn, I'm falling off, I thought to myself, as I wondered why I never saw her. And so I stared back at her, not really knowing what game we were playing, but not wanting to let her win either. *This is a weird ass bitch!*

Although I wanted to play this petty-ass childish game with her, I realized that time wasn't on my side because I still had things to settle with Oshyn. So I decided to get up to see what this meeting was all about. I walked over to her table and sat down across from her as she took a sip from her Starbucks cup.

"Who are you?" she asked, as she pushed her over-sized Emilio Pucci shades up on her nose, which I assumed was hiding her eyes that I would bet were black. A few bruises and small cuts from the windshield glass lay on her face, and I noticed that the front teeth that had fallen out were now back in place. Despite all of the bang ups her body had endured, she was still sexy.

"So, you got your teeth back?" I asked, ignoring her dumb-ass question. I wanted her to know that I was in control of this and that she would follow my lead.

"They were fake anyway," she said nonchalantly, as she waved her hand in an *I don't care* motion. "Carlos knocked my real ones out years ago when I was twenty-four, so now when he punches me in the mouth, I can normally just pop them right back in."

Damn, I thought, not believing that she was being so candid with me. *I have to watch her. She has something up her sleeve.*

And she continued. "But you never answered my question. Who the fuck are you?" She took another sip of whatever was in her cup and brushed back a few fly away hairs that popped out of her extremely long ponytail with her fingers.

And then waited.

For an answer.

"Who the fuck are *you*?" was my response. She didn't hesitate to give an answer.

"I'm Carlos' wife. The mother of his only son. The woman he chose to spend the rest of his life with until death do us part. That's who the fuck I am. Now, like I said, who the fuck are you, and what are you doing with my husband?"

She grabbed her Louis Vuitton Damier bag and unzipped it, taking out a pack of Newport cigarettes. Shorts. She stuck one in her mouth and then waited again.

For an answer.

I couldn't help but to crack a smile at her. Because she was a comic who didn't realize how funny she actually was. But she was a sloppy comic who hadn't done her homework, because if she had, she would've known who I was and why I was no one to fuck with. This was no secret. It was a known fact that everyone in my city had become accustomed to, and those muthafuckas stayed out of my way.

"Don't make me have to ask you again," Nina said as she lit her cancer stick up, taking a pull, and blowing it in my face. "Who...are...you?"

"I'm the bitch that will kill you while your son watches, and then will stab him to death after you stop breathing. I'm the bitch that will set you on fire, and watch you dance around until you burn to death. I'm the bitch that will bury you alive, and watch in pure pleasure while the last breaths you inhale are dirt. I'm the last of the Mohicans. A true definition

143

of the word gangsta. I'm a killer. A murderer. I do this for fun because I can and nobody will stop me. I fuck who I want, when I want, and right now, it's your *nigga*."

Had to catch my breath before I continued.

"So, before we go any further with this…whatever the fuck this is…watch what you say to me." I paused for a few seconds to let that set in. "I don't know if you chose this spot because it was in public, but be warned that I don't give a fuck where we are. Unlike you, I don't shoot and miss." I put a smile back on my face, extended my hand and said, "It's a pleasure to meet you."

Expecting her to say something else smart, I was very surprised when she extended her hand and shook mine. It was something I definitely didn't expect after my monologue of threats I had just issued.

"So, what's up?" I asked, trying to get to the point of this crap after the awkward icebreaker we had just shared.

"I simply just want to know what the deal is with you and my husband. That bastard won't give me any answers, so I figured we could talk woman to woman to get this shit straight and clear up some of the confusion. How long have you known him?"

"Well, babe, I'm not a woman to woman type of bitch, but I've known him for about a week, and it was love at first sight."

She erupted into laughter. So hard that she inhaled the nicotine down the wrong pipe and began to choke.

"Oh my goodness, now that was some hilarious random shit to say." She stopped to cough a few more times, cleared her throat then continued. "One week? You've known *my* husband for one week and now you're in love? That's that dumb shit they must do up here in Rochester. You ain't no real New York bitch!"

"Nah, boo, this is that dumb shit we do here in Rochester."

I grabbed an old, used plastic knife that hadn't been thrown away from the last person, and without thinking twice, slid my hand under the table and rammed it into her thigh. Her cries of pain startled the few people that were actually eating, as I warned her to shut up.

"I'm a Roc bitch for life, and don't you ever forget it," I stated.

She continued to moan in agony, as I took the bloody knife out of her skin and placed it back on the table. Small evidence of what I was capable of, and what I would do again if she said some more slick shit out her mouth.

But she didn't budge.

Didn't get up and storm out like I had assumed she would, but then again deep down inside I knew she was going to stay. Any woman that had her teeth knocked out *often* wouldn't let a simple plastic knife wound stop her. She was a woman with a purpose, and who wasn't going to leave until she got what she came here for.

Her husband.

"I'm sorry," she confessed. For the first time since I sat down, I had calmed down enough to hear her thick New York City accent. It amazed me that, although we were from the same state, we sounded nothing alike. There was no common ground between the city and upstate New York, and personally, I was glad.

Upstate niggas got slept on.

The NYC boys came up here and got put to sleep for life.

"I know you don't have anything at all to do with this, but I just had my son. He's not even a month old, and this nigga is out here fucking you. He left me for you," she said confused, with a hint of disgust in her voice. And then she continued. "I mean, after all I've done for him. I bailed his sorry-ass out of jail, and that shit was so high it took me and three of my aunts to put houses up to get him released. And he still ain't paid them back yet. He was broke not too long ago, and I'm the one who put his ass back on, and now he wants to leave me?"

"Look, I don't argue well, so what is the point of this?

What are you trying to say? From what you're saying, Carlos seems like he doesn't want to fuck with you or your son anymore, so you probably just need to move on with your life."

"No," she said defiantly, as she shook her head from side to side. "My family will be back together. If that's the last thing I do, we will be happy again, and he's going to come back home, whether he wants to or not."

I took note of how beautiful she was as I watched her talk. Fight for her family, which was the same thing I had done. Only I meant it. Nina was a woman scorned; one that would say absolutely anything to break up the new foundation that we had built.

"He's not over me though," she continued, snapping me out of my thoughts. "He'll never let me go. That's why I had his cell phone and called you from it while he was sleeping. Hard. After I put this pussy on him. He's use to me following him around from state to state. This isn't anything new. He thrives on the drama. Loves it."

While she kept talking, I wondered why I had allowed her to continue. I would have drug this girl up and down this food court by now, but something in me wouldn't let me. Maybe it had to do with the gypsy's prediction of love. Maybe it was my desire to actually be in it, but I knew that he was the one. Yeah, one week is no time to get to know someone, but he had already proved himself in murdering my ex. So, she couldn't be telling the truth.

"I can prove it," she said. "Come with me back to my hotel. He'll be meeting me there in a couple of hours after the concert to talk. To make up for his abuse like he always does. To give me a portion of the little bit of money he made. You can be hiding in the closet. To listen. To know for a fact that this isn't your man. That he misses me. That he's coming back home, and you can let go before this gets ugly."

My mind was stuck on her words, *what little bit of money he made*. "He makes a lot of money. I know personally. I watched him splurge on me."

She laughed, then shook her head. "Chick, it's all a

146

game. And you're obviously slow. He's spending his bosses' money."

"He is the boss!" I snapped. I threw my hand to her face. Simply didn't want to hear anymore lies. I wasn't stupid, she was trying to manipulate my mind.

"I just want my husband back," Nina blurted out. "I want you to see that he still wants me too."

I didn't respond.

We both stared at each other strangely, wanting the same man. Like me and Oshyn had done not too long ago.

"Fine, I'll go," I agreed.

Nina smiled, rubbed her hands together and said, "Let the games begin."

Chapter Twenty
(Chloe)

Another hotel.

This time Nina's.

I sat secretly with my mouth shut in the darkness of her hotel closet Indian style. Like a fucking kid in nursery school, I sat with the double doors shut tightly. The crack between the doorway was my only connection to what was going on in the room. Every now and then I could see Nina prance past me half-naked, wearing a pair of black laced, v-string thongs with the matching bra. It was killing me not being in control. Not being in the mix. She looked good, good enough to eat, but I wasn't ready to go back to my lesbian days just yet. Besides, my instructions were to wait for Carlos to arrive. I tapped my fingers on the closet floor, while becoming more impatient by the minute. I couldn't wait for that nigga to show up so I could either blast him or prove to Nina that she was wrong about my man. It was official. I *was* in love and ready to admit it to the world. But I didn't take too kindly to relationship betrayal. For both of their sake, hopefully Nina was wrong.

Time seemed to pass slowly, but when I checked the time on my cell, it read 4:00 p.m. So, on the real, things were moving rather quickly. I knew I had to get back to Oshyn, but had already equated Carlos as equally important. Nina had R. Kelly's old tunes playing throughout the room via her Ipod speaker. *Twelve Play* had just come on, sending me into a frenzy. I sung the lyrics, getting aroused second by second. I sang to myself, and watched Nina as best I could as she sexily swayed across the floor. If I didn't know better I would've thought she was purposefully trying to tease me.

Her body was incredible. Sculpted like Michelangelo had created her himself. Her figure was deceiving underneath her original clothing, but after seeing her in just her bra and panties, I was willing to bet she lifted light weights. I wasn't sure what else she did, but I knew I had to break free from my temporary hiding place.

I just wanted to feel her breasts.

In my mouth.

I stood up boldly, broke through the closet doors, and walked right up on Nina, grabbing her by her hair. She looked surprised, almost wanting to ask me my reasoning for not hiding anymore.

"Damn, you're sexy," I told her.

I expected a response, but got an unexpected advance in return. Then it happened. Her delicate lips touched mine as she pulled me close to her perky 36C breasts. It was a feeling that I had never felt with a man. No nigga on the streets could do what she was doing to me. My feelings started going wild, my thoughts first, then my hormones. Unlike Nina, who kept her focus by driving her tongue inside my mouth, then encircling my lips artfully with her tongue.

Her artistic talent started at the top with my lips, then made her way down to my belly-button, where she stopped and pulled my tunic shirt above my head. I played the submissive role and let her do her thing. I knew Carlos was on the way, but I was a selfish bitch. If I could sneak an orgasm and then tell him nothing happened, that worked for me. I wasn't sure what Nina had up her sleeve, but I wanted to get licked. Ate out like people do when eating watermelon at family reunions.

I guess I threw her off guard when I reached down, unzipped my own pants, and pulled them off, along with my thongs. She smiled then stepped back to size me up. My bra was the only garment left, and it didn't matter since Nina had gone full steam ahead. A sense of newness filled me as she pushed me onto the bed and spread my legs apart like a wide V. Without hesitation she dove inside, head first, making love to my clit.

As she licked, sucked and spat, my muscles contracted. It felt so damn good. "Damn, Nina," was all I could say. I wanted to scream, but tried hard to hold it inside. Before I knew it, she started this thing where she kept flicking her tongue like a snake. The kind you want in your home. The kind you want in your bed. "Oh, shit!" I belted, then grinded my ass all in her face. "Eat this pussy, Nina. It's yours. It's yoursssssss," I told her, prolonging the sound of the letter *s*.

I started rubbing my hands all over the top part of her head, the farthest I could reach, until she pushed me further up the bed and drilled her tongue inside my hole. I started moaning, and my eyeballs rolled up into my head. The time had come.

Then came the knock.

The knock at the door we both had been waiting for.

Abruptly Nina stopped. I grabbed the bitch by the ear, dragging her back down toward my pussy. She pushed me away as if we were a victim. And I was holding her hostage to bless my clit.

"Later," she told me, with a seductive grin. "I want you to see Carlos in action. "You gotta stop believing niggas," she warned.

Pissed off, I retreated back to the closet, and closed the door behind me. I had forgotten my shirt on the floor near the foot of the bed, but didn't give a good fuck. My hormones

151

were raging and I needed to cum. Bad.

Nina's nasty-ass had made it to the door and let Carlos in by the time I had calmed myself down. I couldn't see him at first, but could only hear his voice. I knew the room smelled like pussy, but wondered if he smelled it too. Typical nigga, he just walked around sniffing, then took his shoes off.

I jumped back and placed my hand on my heart at the thought of him getting comfortable. I expected him to be beefing with Nina, or asking her why she called him there. Instead, Nina jump started the conversation.

"I've been waiting for you, sexy," Nina said seductively.

"Man, Nina, you bi-polar. Sometimes we friends, other times you don't wanna even talk to me."

"That's not true, Los," she called him, and placed her hands around his shoulder. I was pissed. Thought that was my pet name exclusively for me and him to use. Nina began to massage him, standing almost two feet lower than him. "You know the relationship between us has been rough lately. But just know that I still love you."

The nigga grinned. "You do?" he questioned.

"I do. In spite of everything. I wanna prove it to you," she added.

His eyes grew to the size of an eight ball. "Like we fucking?" he asked.

"Of course. You think I did all this for nothing?" Nina asked as she pranced around, modeling for my man. Her husband. Carlos wasted no time.

"Dirty muthafucka," I said under my breath. I had my fist balled up while I watched him set the Guinness World Book of Records for the fastest man to undress.

Before I knew it, he had scooted up behind Nina and said, "You know we got to use a condom. I got one in the front pocket of my pants."

"Get it, nigga," she erupted, accompanied by the crinkling of her forehead.

Ass-naked Carlos slid the condom on, and before it

got secure, it popped open. Ignoring the fact that the condom had broken, he peeled the remaining pieces off, threw it on the floor and grabbed Nina from behind. He took a few baby steps, positioning himself closer to the bed, almost wanting to place himself for the actual fuck fest. Pulling her tightly, he yanked her with force until her ass set firmly against his stiff dick. Carlos commenced to kissing at the back of her neck, while my blood continued to boil. Nina was right. Another nigga bites the dust. I wasn't about to let the lovebirds fuck. At least if the relationship was over, I wanted to get mine.

I opened the doors to the closet slowly, expecting Carlos to turn my way. Unfortunately, for him, he was so in the Nina zone that he never looked behind him. His firm ass stared me in the face, and I wished I had a knife at that moment. I sucked it up and made my move.

I came up behind him, saying, "I'm so glad you could make it, Carlos."

He heard my voice, and without turning around mumbled, "Chloe?"

"Yes, it's me, nigga," I said, in the softest voice I could muster.

"What…what…what…"

"Cat got your tongue, nigga? It was just on Nina's neck. And hers was just on my pussy."

He couldn't respond.

Nina couldn't either.

She was probably wondering why I had defaulted on the plan. That was what I did. Never followed the ruled. She also probably thought about the consequences Carlos would put on her now that he knew she had to be the one to let me in. I removed my bra, the only piece of clothing between us all, and threw it across the bed.

We all stood in a single file line, naked, Carlos behind Nina and me behind him. He was still in a state of trauma. And it was made clear by the way his dick went limp. I continued to stay in line, grabbing him around the waist and resting my head on his back. I couldn't see his eyes, but could tell he didn't know what to do. The nigga had been caught ready to stick his dick in Nina. But I wasn't about to let that happen. He would fuck me. And Nina would make me feel good too. I knew she was down. The horny expression on her face showed it.

"Since you want to fuck, Carlos. How about we all fuck?" I asked him boldly.

Stunned, his voice cracked. "You…sure…Chloe?"

I'm positive," I said, moving from behind him and rushing over to rub Nina along the crack of her ass.

She smiled, showing her approval, and commenced to massaging my tits. Carlos' expression spoke for his feelings. He was stunned but ready and willing. Wide-eyed, he tugged at his shit, hoping to get it to its ten inches again.

"I'm fucking him first," Nina emitted.

"Says who?" I bent quickly to lick his shit like a lollipop, while Nina tasted the crack of my ass.

It was a threesome, yet a competition all in one. "Oh, no the hell you not," I told her, after tasting the appetizer. I stood straight up ready to ride Carlos, but Nina was already on it. She ordered Carlos to sit, and within seconds went to work on his knob. She slobbered and slobbered, while Carlos reared back with his hands gripping the comforter of the bed. Nina had her knees on the floor, while I positioned myself on the floor and commenced to licking her clit. I kept teasing her…stopping then starting again. Besides, I was envious of the way she made my man moan. Jealousy traveled through my veins as my nose began to spread.

I wasn't having it and couldn't play along. I hopped up, knocked Nina out of the way, and threw myself onto the bed. I rolled onto my back and cocked my legs high in the air, staring at Carlos with a threatening look. He knew what time it was. Within seconds, he had hopped onto the bed and onto my sweaty body. He thrust himself into my wetness like I was the only woman on earth, causing me to forgive the fact that he was gonna fuck Nina.

The nigga was working me overtime, trying to cram every ounce of dick up in me. He grinded hard and I pushed back as he dug deeper. At that moment, the bitch Nina got clever. She rushed us out of nowhere, sitting on her knees right beside Carlos. Before I knew it, she'd arched her back and positioned her neatly shaven pussy directly in view for Carlos to see.

"Eat it," she begged.

He took one lick, ready to feast until I yanked at his arms, showing my resistance. I couldn't believe while he was on top of me working my walls, she wanted to steal the show. A show stopper Nina would not be. I was the only bitch who could do shit like that.

I changed shit up.

I pressed against Carlos' chest, signaling him to get off of me. It was my turn to ride. Nina was still on her knees, looking at me like a pitiful child. I smiled at her then kissed her ferociously in the mouth. I saw Carlos slide under me, showing me that he knew what was up. I wanted him on his back for me to take control. Suddenly, I rammed his stiff dick inside of me and started riding him slowly at first. Nina had me mesmerized by the way she switched up her flow. She remained on the bed, still on her knees, biting at my hardened nipples and French kissing me in the mouth.

My movements on top of Carlos quickened as I felt an orgasm headed to the surface. I started bucking like a disgruntled bull, asking him to give me more.

"More, more!" I shouted, while working my pussy on his thick dick.

I pushed my shit as far as it would go onto Carlos' manhood. I wanted to explode but had some more riding to do. Hours if possible. My chances of Carlos holding out for me to get my nut off were slim. The nerves in his dick jumped like crazy, as Nina kept encircling my nipples with her tongue. We were fucking like jack rabbits, calling out over the music in the room.

Then it happened.

Nina had something to say. Her face was bawled up and had turned a bright reddish color.

"Chloe, one thing I forgot to tell you."

I just looked at her real-crazy like. Wondering what made her think I would stop, or even raise up off the dick.

"Carlos has AIDS," she told me wickedly.

Chapter Twenty-One
(Chloe)

Before I was able to get his big diseased dick out of me, Carlos grabbed Nina's throat with his strong hand that was big enough to palm a basketball. Trying to break free, her big pierced titties swung around as he choked her ferociously. And Nina struggled to suck up any available air. I watched, wishing that it were my hands who were causing her pain. Wishing it were my hands that were squeezing all of the life that was in her body out of it. A beautiful thick body that would go to waste in just a few seconds like my girlfriend Joy's had done only a few years ago.

Déjà vu.

Is what my life had become.

Her words, *Carlos has Aids,* ran across my mind over and over again while I watched them fight.

"You fucking bitch!" were the continuous rambles that he spat at his wife. A woman who he once loved. A woman that he now despised. All of her scratches and punches went unnoticed, until one of her nails caught his eye and he suddenly let go of her neck, like a wounded puppy would to tend to his injury.

She coughed.

157

And then gagged.

And then inhaled as much air as she could, trying to recoup all of it that was lost.

"He didn't tell you?" she asked, as she punched him in the same eye that he was wounded in. "He cheated on me, brought that incurable shit into my home, and into my son's life!" Tears exploded out of her eyes as she found the strength to continue. "And I forgave him. Because that's what you do for love. Because he was my husband, and because I made a vow to never leave, no matter what!"

"She's lying!" he managed to say between his constant groans. "I don't have anything!"

He continued to press his palm against his eye, somehow hoping that the pressure would take the pain away. But I was sure that it was only making the problem worse.

"You lying bastard!" she screamed, after taking her foot and ramming it into his balls. "You didn't even have the balls to tell me about it yourself. You made the doctor tell me while your bitch-ass sat in the chair crying, apologizing because you stole my son's future from us before he was even born."

While they went on with their family issues, I slipped away to the corner of the room and put on my clothes, still trying to wrap my head around the fact that this dude had HIV and stuck his dick inside of me raw. They continued to argue while I watched and I was so confused and angry that I had become numb.

So numb that I couldn't feel the anger that slowly began to mount in my heart. So numb that I couldn't feel the urge to murder. I had become so numb that I didn't feel myself walking over to the wide glass bottle of Patron Platinum, picking it up, and pouring the Tequila all over her naked body.

"What in the hell are you doing?" she asked, as she switched her focus from her disease riddled husband to me.

I took the lighter that sat where the bottle of Patron

once was and lit it. Answering her question. The dancing orange flame barely grazed her skin before it took over and met with the Tequila, engulfing her up in flames. The screams that escaped out of her mouth didn't even sound human as she danced around, trying her best to put the fire out.

Not able to tell if he was happy with the fact that I had finally gotten her to shut up, or mad that I had gotten rid of his wife for life, Carlos remained emotionless, that was until she ran toward him. The sound of the fire alarm and the smell of burning flesh filled the room as she melted away, and when she reached him, he quickly kicked her away, not wanting to risk the chance of catching fire himself. Now that bitch could feel the pain I felt when I was on fire. Somebody needed to feel that pain.

The sprinkler system finally caught wind of the danger I had started in the room, and the water poured down over us. Nina's body lay on the ground as the fire died down, and Carlos threw on his clothes in record time.

"Help me" and "I love you," were words I thought I heard slip out of Nina's mouth, while Carlos finished up by putting his shoes on.

"Get the fuck up and come on. We gotta get out of here!" he demanded, as he quickly headed toward the door.

"You don't want to kiss her goodbye?" I asked sarcastically, as I quickly followed him out.

He never answered.

Never looked behind him, to see if his other half was okay, before shutting the door on her freshly burned body.

By the time we reached his car, three fire trucks had flooded the parking lot and the firefighters ran out of their vehicles suited up and ready to do their jobs. Carlos had sparked up another joint and began smoking it. He was obviously disturbed as he pulled on the brown blunt unusually hard. We sat in his car in silence for several minutes, not wanting to look suspicious, until he decided to start it up. Purple haze filled the new rental car he had gotten, which didn't mix with the new car scent that the car already smelled like.

I cracked the window.

Needed to breathe.

"What the fuck were you doing in Nina's hotel room anyway?" Not sure why that was the first question he thought to ask, but I assumed that he just recalled the fact that I had come out of the closet and not through the front door.

"What the fuck was I doing in there?" I repeated. "What the fuck were *you* doing in there?"

We questioned each other *as if* we had been a couple since adolescence. *As if* it hadn't been only a week since we first met. We questioned each other *as if* we weren't actually strangers, and I watched him scratch his head *as if* he were trying to come up with an answer.

"She said that you had AIDS. AIDS!" I yelled, trying to stop the throw up that began to come up my throat.

"I don't have AIDS…"

"HIV muthafucka! Don't act like you don't know what the hell I'm talking about!"

"I don't have that shit either. I don't have anything, no STDs, nothing. That stupid-ass bitch was lying to you! She just wanted to make you mad. She just wanted to ruin my life."

I stared at him with my gut instinct trying to warn me that the words that fell off his tongue were all lies. My instincts screamed in my ear, telling me not to trust him, telling me to kill him and get rid of the body. And then I stared at him, trying to figure out why I wanted to believe him. Trying to find the turning point in my life where my desire to be loved overrode my desire to kill. And then my mind cruised back to the words of the gypsy. A strange old woman whose words had instantly changed my life.

"I have to get the fuck out of this town," Carlos said, as he inhaled the last of the thick smoke and then put out the rest of his blunt. "The money I came here to make just isn't worth it."

I thought about what Nina told me before I spoke confidently. "Carlos, I know all about you and how you make your money. It's not even yours," I said sadly.

"Don't believe what you hear. I do have partners," he admitted. "We split the money, and it's normally good," he lied. "We've just been taking losses."

When Carlos couldn't look me in the face, I knew Nina must've told me the truth. He was probably a worker. A damn flunkie. Someone I didn't want or need.

He continued to rant. "Two people have been murdered in this city that my face can be tied to. Shit that will put me away for life. I just can't risk staying here. I'm going to leave. Now!"

"What about me?" I asked, not hearing anything about *us* in his plans.

"Are you serious? Absolutely none of this shit would've happened to me if I hadn't met you. Nothing has gone right since you came in the picture. I mean, it's as if the world came tumbling down the moment I laid my eyes on you."

He said it.

Crushing the high hopes I had for us recklessly with his words.

Contradicting the fortune telling promise I received of the true love that would come into my life. But I knew just how to solve it. He would die just like the rest of them. Just like everyone else who had hurt my heart and betrayed my trust. Carlos no longer got a pardon for being "the one", and I was going to teach him a very valuable lesson. That, I, Chloe Rodriguez, wasn't meant to be fucked with.

I shifted around in my seat with the tension of stress creeping up my spine, as I began brainstorming quick ways to kill him. Although I would have preferred him to die a long, torturous death like I had planned for Oshyn, I still had my obligation to get back to her and finish her off.

She was more important.

It was personal.

"But there's something about you that won't let me leave you alone," he said, interrupting my thoughts of ending his life. "It's like we were meant to be." He drove off in a daze, in an attempt to figure everything out. He had somewhat put my mind at ease, and for the moment, his execution had been stayed. "I want you to come with me."

Elated to hear his change of heart, I had once again become the schoolgirl who had her first crush. "But where would we go?" I asked, not really caring.

"It doesn't matter. I have to go get my son first, but we could move out of the country. Start over. Raise a family."

All of that sounded really good and all, but the thought of raising Nina's son as mine really left a bad taste in my mouth. The baby would be interference in my master plan, and would quite possibly, at times, come first. His son would remind Carlos of his wife, and even if he didn't say it, I knew that he would miss her occasionally. A risk I couldn't take.

I would find a way to get the little bastard out of our lives permanently, even if it took killing him off. But he wouldn't miss him for long because I would give him plenty sons of my own.

And a daughter.

Just one.

And we would raise our family just as Brooklyn and Oshyn did. In another country. Making money somehow illegally. I began to tingle with joy at the mere thought of finally being someone's wife, and I would protect my family until my death. Not like Oshyn had done by letting me kill them all off. But she was no one to be compared to. She was always a scared-ass bitch. Never had balls. Always borrowed mine.

"You don't have to bring anything," he said, as he jumped on the highway. "I'm going to go straight to the city now, pick lil man up, and we can book a flight from there."

This dude has it all planned out, I thought, as I admired his ability to think ahead. And then it hit me. Like a ton of bricks.

"I can't go right now. I just have one more thing to do. Let's leave first thing in the morning, okay?"

"One more thing? We'll be in jail *before* first thing in the morning comes, and going by your fucking track record, someone else will be dead."

And oh how right he was.

Oshyn was still a priority, and I needed to go back and finish the business I had started with her and the kids before I left town. Although I wanted to make her torture long and painful, with the new plans, I was going to have to speed it up if I wanted to squeeze the kids in with it. There were no if ands or butts about it. The deed had to be done before I left for Rochester, New York.

"This is important. If this is my last time here, I have to finish this. Turn this car around and take me back to my car," I said, remembering that it was still in the hotel parking deck.

"Don't you ever watch the movies? All the major king-pins got caught because they had to make one more move before they quit the drug game forever. Their one more move always landed them with a life sentence or death. I can't risk that. I'm not turning around."

As much as I wanted a chance at raising my own family, my desire to get revenge for everything Oshyn had done to me was bigger. An addiction that I was sure would lead to my demise, but it was a risk I was willing to take. I grabbed the steering wheel that he had such a tight hold on and yanked it to the left, swerving it into the next lane, causing the other drivers to honk their horns repeatedly.

"What the fuck are you doing, stupid bitch!" Carlos yelled.

"Take me back to my car!" I screamed like I was going insane. "Take me back now!" I warned one more time before I took a yank at his wheel again, causing it, this time, to go over the grates that make all that noise. He slapped me so hard it knocked me back on my side of the car.

Where I originally was.

Where I was originally supposed to be.

And just as he was about to swing on me again, sirens went off behind us. An unmarked black Charger was the cause of all the racket, and with all the swerving our car had done into other lanes, and the sweet smell of weed that still lingered in the air, I couldn't think of any other choice but to run.

Chapter Twenty-Two
(Chloe)

"Oh shit, look what *you* did!" Carlos said panicking. His foot never let up on the pedal as I watched the stick on the speedometer rise to one hundred miles per hour.

"Me?" I asked, as I pointed my hand roughly against my chest. "How the fuck is any of this my fault?"

"You should've kept your hands to yourself. If you would've never taken the steering wheel and jerked the car around, the police wouldn't be in the back of us now. Its broad daylight out here, what in the hell were you thinking? It's your fault the reason they're behind us. If it's not one thing, it's the next fucking with you!"

I turned around and noticed another police car had decided to join the party. This one was marked. He was trailing behind the unmarked Charger, and both were keeping a steady speed on us.

"It's like you have a curse on you or something," he added as he rolled down his window, trying to release the scent of purple haze out of the car. As if that was going to stop the inevitable.

His arrest.

He was now tipping over one hundred and ten miles per hour, and if nothing else, they were going to arrest him for running from the law, which was something I had done all of my life. And got away with. Paranoia had replaced his high, as he struggled to come to terms with the fact that this may have been the end for him.

"I can't even fucking believe that I got caught up with a bitch like you. You ruined my whole life. My whole fucking life!"

I sat in my seat and soaked all of his words in. *This muthafucka doesn't even realize how lucky he really is,* I thought, as I desperately began wishing that I got the chance to show him how I really got down.

"I can't believe that the police…"

"Shut the fuck up about them! Believe me, if you knew how a bitch like me got down, you would know that they are the least of your worries."

"Who do you think you're talking to? You shut the fuck up before I knock all the teeth out of your mouth like Nina. And you know what, as a matter of fact, when all of this blows over, I'm going to beat the shit out of you."

"Do you know who you're dealing with? Do I look like your bitch-ass wife?" I asked, before punching him on the side of his face. He took one hand off the steering wheel, and before he had a chance to raise it in an attempt to strike me back, I warned him about our company.

"I'm going to kill you," was what he grumbled under his breath, as he rubbed his jaw and lowered his hand back on the wheel.

I remained calm, because in all actuality, I had no other choice. Any other reaction from me would've been deadly for him and fatal for my future, so I had to stay in a place where I was going to make decisions that was going to safely get me out of this car and back to Oshyn.

Carlos continued to worry and complain as I kicked myself in the ass, wondering what made me detour from my initial mission. While I was in the hospital recovering from Oshyn and Brooklyn's attempts to end my life, the only thoughts that ran through my mind were her demise. I just

166

couldn't figure out how I let a random nigga slip in and take me off of my game. This was the second time in my life where I had been a sucka for love. I hit myself in the fore-head, vowing to never let that happen again.

"You gotta be kidding me," he said suddenly.

"What?"

"There's not enough gas. I'm running out of gas!" Car-los said in a panic, as he pointed to the gas light that had just lit up. He banged his head violently on the wheel, while he spat out a few more curse words. "How could I have for-gotten to get the fucking gas?"

I chuckled.

Inappropriate.

Long.

Awkward.

My laugh was so out of place that even he was lost for words concerning its cause, but there was a reason for my strange outburst.

I laughed to keep myself from going insane. To stop myself from thinking that I'd never get to finish Oshyn off, and that the possibility that she would live longer than today might've been possible all because his stupid-ass didn't have enough gas in the tank to get away.

Who did that dumb shit?

On a high speed chase?

And then I thought that maybe he was right. Maybe I was cursed and the dust that the gypsy blew on me solidified my downfall, promising to make everything I put my hands on crumble. But I quickly dismissed the idea, because shit never went right in my life, starting with my mother, whom I missed dearly. It was at that very moment that I realized that the curse didn't come from the old scary looking woman in Saint Tropez. It came from my family.

A generational curse.

That lived alive and strong in me.

"I'm gonna have to pull over," he confessed, as bullets of sweat began to pop out of his pores.

"For what? You have about forty more miles until the car actually stops running. The gas light is just a warning sign. Just make a couple sharp turns and lose their asses," I said, wishing that a little common sense would hit him in the head.

"Nah, that's too risky. We're going to tell the police that you were in an accident and we had to get you to the hospital for an emergency. A heart attack. When we pull over tell the cops that you thought you were having a heart attack."

"You have to be the stupidest person alive!" I replied, as I listened to the explanation that he thought was going to get him off. "A heart attack? Really? Who is going to believe that nonsense, and even if they did, we passed two hospitals already."

I rolled my eyes at his foolish idea. An idea that I wasn't going to follow through with, even if it did make sense, because I was getting out of this mess. I couldn't risk not being believed by the police and taken into custody for something as little as questioning.

Today, Carlos would be left on his own.

Like I had been all of my life.

"Just…just go with the story. That's all *we* have is this story. And you," he said, turning his head to look at me. "You owe me!"

I rolled my eyes about him using the word *we*, and I rolled them even harder at his assumption that I owed him anything. I had paid my debts to this fucked up society, and didn't owe anyone a muthafuckin' thing.

"Did you hear me?" Carlos asked, in response to my silence. He released his foot off the gas, slowing down the speed of his car tremendously, and repeated himself. "Did…you…fucking…hear…me?"

"Yes, baby, I heard you," I answered back, as I reached over and placed my hand on his damp thigh. A place where his stream of perspiration had also found its way to. He looked at me with a hint of unsettlement in his

168

eyes, as he wondered why I had all of a sudden become nice. Gentle.

"I don't know how we met, and I don't even know why we met, but none of this was by chance. The one week that we have gotten to know each other feels like we've been in a ten year relationship. It's as if we're glued together. A lot of chances to just walk away from each other have come and gone, where we would never see each other again, but we chose to stay."

I paused to let my words sink in as I watched his heavy breathing calm down. "I'm a ride or die bitch, and I'm going to stick with you no matter what happens. We're going to make it out of this, and I want to be by your side when we do."

I felt the tension in his body soften up, while my sweet nothings in his ear soothed his mind, reassuring him that everything was going to be okay. When the car slowed down to about twenty miles per hour we heard the grates sing as he eased it into the pull over lane.

And then it stopped.

Abruptly.

For the first time since the whole ordeal began my heart started to race. Just the mere thought of none of this working out was enough to make me throw up. *This can't be it*, I thought to myself, as I caught a glimpse of the three officers walking toward us and all with their guns drawn. *This can't be how my life is supposed to end.*

"Just stay calm," he reminded me with a slight smile painted on his face, trying to convince me that everything was going to be okay. Something he couldn't guarantee himself.

"Put your hands on the steering wheel!" was what came pounding out one of the officers' mouth as they reached the car. "And don't you move fucker, or I'll blow your damn head off!" I knew that that wasn't proper procedure, but the police around here did whatever they wanted to do anyway. That's just how shit was.

169

"Officer, I can explain," Carlos cried, as he switched his demeanor from a hood nigga to...one of them. "Please, it's an emergency. My girlfriend thinks that she is having a heart attack. She has a bad heart, and I need to get her to the hospital as soon as possible. I couldn't afford to stop for you guys because I just didn't want her to die."

"That doesn't make any sense because you just sped past two hospitals before pulling over here," one of the officers pointed out.

"Yeah, but I'm not from here and I was in a panic. She wasn't talking, but now that you mention it, I recall her pointing several times, trying to get me to see something, but I just had no idea what to do. There was so much confusion. You all were following me, I'm not a criminal, she was dying...I just didn't know what to do. I still need to get her to the Emergency Room though. Time is of the essence."

I had to admit it, Carlos was good, so good that the officers' aggressiveness had simmered down a little bit. So good that I grasped my heart to see if there was still a steady beat, and worried when it seemed to pound rapidly. So good, that for the first time, I thought that we had a good chance of getting out of this mess.

"Please, officer, you can lead the way so we can get there faster, and I can give you all of my information when we arrive, but we can't just sit here. We have to get her some kind of help."

He took my hand and squeezed it, assuring me again that he had everything all under control.

"Ma'am," another officer said, as he tapped on my window, "can you please roll this window down?"

I followed his instructions and pressed the button that sat on the armrest. A nice breeze floated from outside and grazed my cheekbone, as the man with the badge looked at me with sympathy.

"Are you okay?" he asked.

I ignored him.

Looked forward as if he wasn't speaking to me. As if

our lives didn't depend on a simple yes or no answer.

"Ma'am, I just asked you a question. Are you okay?" I could tell in his voice that the ease he once had quickly slipped away, as he placed his fingers on the unlatched gun that sat on his hip.

"Baby, answer him. Tell him the truth, that everything is *not* okay and that you need to get some help *now*. Tell him what he wants to hear," Carlos pleaded with me, worried about the fact that I was going to fuck up the masterpiece he had just created.

And he was right.

I couldn't risk his master plan not working, and no matter how close we seemed to be free, it just wasn't close enough. Just the thought of me not being able to feel this breeze was intolerable.

"No, I'm not okay," I responded. Carlos breathed a sigh of relief as I continued. "I'm being held against my will! I'm not having a heart attack, but he told me that he would kill me if I didn't play along!"

"You stupid bitch!" Carlos screamed, as my body served as a punching bag to his heavy punches.

"Help me!" I screamed, as it took all of the officers to pull him off of me. "He killed him. He's the guy that murdered that man at the funeral home, and he just set his wife on fire at the Ramada Inn on Jefferson Road not even twenty minutes ago."

"She's lying!" Carlos belted, trying his best to break the hold they had on him. "That bitch is a fucking liar!"

"I tried to get away. Tried to call you all for help, but he wouldn't let me. I saw what he did. Twice. I watched how he set the woman he promised to love and cherish up in flames, and I believed him when he said that he would do the same to me."

Tears poured out of my eyes, as one of the officers pulled me to the side in an attempt to console me. Even with his handcuffs on, the other officers continued to tussle with Carlos, as he proved that he wasn't going to give up without

171

a fight. The guy that sat by my side excused himself to help his colleagues, and I was left alone.

Leaning against Carlos's car.

With the ignition still on.

When I felt like everyone was engrossed in calming their suspect of two unsolved murders down, I ran to the driver side of the car, opened up the door and jumped in.

"Hey, stop…" was all I heard, as I cranked up the ignition and drove away with just enough gas to get me to the place that was most important. To the place I had no business leaving from in the first place. Back to Oshyn, where I belonged.

Chapter Twenty-Three
(Oshyn)

"Mommy...Ma...wake up!"

His voice had changed, and he was beginning to sound like a young man. As if he had one of those dreams that transformed boys to men and woke up wet overnight.

"Mom, I said wake up!"

I slowly opened up my eyes and was greeted by my first born son, Micah, who showed nothing but teeth as he smiled at me. His presence was warm. His touch missed.

I let the words, "Micah," slip out of my mouth, as I brushed my finger along his soft chocolate face. "Mommy missed you so much."

"I missed you too," he admitted, as he giggled innocently. "Come with me." He grabbed my hand and began leading me into the light. I took a few steps and then slowed down until I stopped. "Come on!" he demanded, as his little strong hands tugged on mine a little bit harder.

"Wait, where are you taking me?"

"With me," he answered, with a bit of an attitude. Very defensive, like I should've known the answer to my own question. Like I should not have questioned him at all.

"Baby, you have to tell me where you're going? Where does that light lead to?" I shielded my eyes from its brightness.

He looked down.

Never answering my question.

"You are *my* mommy. You *have* to come and live with me now!" He had begun to pout as children so selfishly do.

"Where are Mye and Bella?" I asked curiously, wondering why I didn't see them anywhere around.

Micah and Bella were best friends, soul mates. The kind that would've gotten married when they were only in their twenties. I just found it odd that he was without her. And I was sure that his little brother, Mye Storie, whom he had never met before, would have been in his arms. Showing him the ropes of life as big brothers do, but the kids weren't there.

Just him.

And I found that odd.

"Micah, where are Bella and Mye?" I asked again.

"Who cares? You're with me now and we're together again. They don't matter anymore. Come on!"

He pulled my arm harder than before, refusing to let me disappear out of his life once again. My prince had become so determined.

"I can't go with you, baby. Mommy loves you, but I just can't go. It's not my time," I confessed, as it finally sunk in as to where I was. The afterlife.

"But what about me?" he whined, as he started to cry. Despite his deepened voice, he was still too young to understand the choice that I had to make.

I kneeled down to kiss him on the forehead, and then wrapped him in my arms. "Please understand. I know it's hard, but your Aunt Chloe is trying to hurt them really, really bad. I have to save them. I have to stop her."

He held on tighter, ignoring my pleas for help. Ignoring my pleas to allow me to save a life. He didn't care because no one had saved his. We cried together as we embraced.

"I have to go now," I said.

His grip got tighter.

Suffocated me.

"Micah, I have to go," I repeated.

He wouldn't listen.

Closed his eyes tighter.

"Let me go!" I said forcefully, as I pried his arms from around me. It took a while for me to get them apart, but I finally did, and before I thought twice, I turned around and walked away.

From the light.

And my son.

I couldn't bear to look at his face a moment longer. Couldn't bear to witness the sadness that lived in his eyes because I might have changed my mind and stayed.

"I love you," were the last words I said before I entered into complete blackness.

"Where am I?" I asked as I came to.

I was greeted by a painfully pounding head and a constant flickering movement that seemed to be stuck in my mind, the taste of blood stained my tongue, and a burning feeling on the corner of my eye and lip.

I was fucked up.

I looked around and saw the steel table that housed all the contents that I initially put together to kill her with, but she overpowered me and was now in control, however, she was nowhere around.

"Help, help…help…help!" I screamed into the empty warehouse, as I listened helplessly while the echoes bounced off the walls. "Hhheeeellllllpppp!"

No answer.

Not that I expected one.

My hands were still tied together, and I tried my best to unravel them, but nothing seemed to work.

175

"Mama…I need you!" I waited for her to come. "Mama, please, tell me what to do!"

No answer.

This one surprised me.

I started to cry, feeling like there was nothing that could be done. I was beginning to lose hope, which didn't matter because I had lost everything else. Hope was, at this point, just a privilege I had gotten use to not having.

"Brooklyn? Micah? Anyone? Help me!"

My cries for help and heavy sobs fell on deaf ears and echoed walls, which didn't comfort me. *It's all over*, a voice whispered in my ears, loud enough to drown out the exercises of roaches activity. *She has the kids and they're dead. It's all over, just give up.*

An image of the kids dead bodies ran across my mind as my cries turned into hyperventilation. Despite the blood that saturated Mye's body, he looked to be asleep, while Bella just laid there with her eyes opened, startled. As if she fought. Hard.

"I'm going to kill you!" I screamed to no one in particular, but directing all of my rage to Chloe. "I'm going to kill you!"

I lowered my head in defeat as I let the words, "God help me," slither out of my mouth. A name I hadn't called on before. It was the only name that could rescue me, and instantly a peace and calmness so strong came over me that I was in awe. The running cockroaches in my ears came to a ceasing halt, and the excruciating pain in my head I was experiencing stopped. Nothing seemed to make sense, and everything had all of sudden become okay.

I realized that if I didn't switch my thinking I was going to die, and that was not the position I wanted to be in. Even though I had a million reasons why I wanted to be dead, I had two reasons to live. God had let me know that they were okay, and that was the voice I chose to listen to.

I wiggled the rope that remained tied around my wrists some more until they became tender. Sore even. I was getting rope burn, but that was the least of my worries. At this point, anything was better than the silence of death. You couldn't wake up from that.

Ten minutes had passed as I worked relentlessly to get them loose, and just when I was about to give up, I hit a turning point and it loosened. Not enough to get my hands free, but enough to sustain the hope I was trying so hard to hold on to. *Just a few more minutes*, I said to myself. *I just need a few...more...minutes.* I worked vigorously to get it off. Even though my skin had become raw, I refused to give up.

But I didn't have a few minutes.

"Oh no," I whispered to myself. I stopped what I was doing when I heard keys clanging together in the not too distant hallway. She was back, and I wasn't prepared. Unable to try any longer, I stopped all movement and lowered my head back down and closed my eyes. I needed for her to think that I was still unconscious.

"Oshyn, my dear," she sang out sarcastically. "You have no fucking idea what it took to get me back to you. I almost didn't make it. I got my pussy sucked, set the bitch that did it on fire, and was in a police chase before it was all over!" With my eyes closed I listened intensely as her feet shuffled around some more. "Me killing your ass must be meant to be."

She laughed.

Passionately.

Arrogantly.

"Oshyn!"

I slowed my breathing a bit so she couldn't tell that I had been active. The last thing I needed was for her to think that I had been awake trying to break out of here.

"Oshyn!"

As her footsteps got closer, I closed my eyes tighter, trying to prepare myself for the worst. I was certain that the longer I held out on answering her, the more that upped my chances of another blow to my head.

And I was right.

The massive pain of her banging me on the top of my head hurt so bad that I had been paralyzed into fear. It hurt so bad that any exhaling and inhaling I did made me tremble. So I stopped and held my breath for as long as I could.

"Oshyn!" she screamed for the third time, and before she could hit me again, I looked up. Slowly. Showing her I was weak and vulnerable. "Good morning sister…so glad that you could finally join us today. I have to admit it, I sort of didn't think you were going to come back to after I left, but hallelujah, you made it through!"

The enthusiasm in her voice disgusted me, as I heard in her voice how happy she was that she had another chance to kill me. All the laughter immediately died down when she asked, "Where is Mye and Bella?"

That was a question I just wasn't going to answer. I kept my mouth closed, as I watched her walk to the table and grab the bottle of acid that I had brought to use on her. She had turned my own weapons of mass destruction on me.

"Sulfuric acid," she read off of the white container. "Now this is going to be fun!" She twisted off the top and walked back over to me. "I'm going to ask you again...where are Mye and Bella?"

"Chloe, please, just leave them alone. They're just children, and have nothing to do with this shit. Your beef is not with them, it's with me."

"Oh, but you're wrong. My beef is with you and everybody that you love. I want you to feel the pain that I've felt all of my life and…"

"Look at me!" I screamed, trying to bring her back into reality. "Just fucking look at me! Doesn't it look like I feel what you feel? You took everyone I had. Everyone that has ever loved me, you've murdered them. You have hurt me more than you can ever imagine. We're even!"

"No. I haven't killed everyone. When I get your raggedy-ass kids good and dead, then my mission will be complete."

"Please…just leave them out of this," I cried out again, hoping she would have mercy on me and hear my pleas.

"Do you know what sulfuric acid does to you?" she asked, quickly changing the subject. She poured a little of it into the bucket of water she tried to drown me in and it started to boil. "If this is what it does to water, what do you think it will do to that soft supple skin of yours?"

She waited for my response.

I said nothing.

"The kids will dissolve away in no time once I pour this over them."

"If you fucking touch those kids I will…"

"You'll what?" she chuckled. "I don't believe that you're in any position to make idle threats now, are you?"

I wasn't.

Mye and Bella were still in the hotel room safe for the moment with my grandmother, but I didn't know how long that was going to last. I couldn't imagine the fact of them being put in the foster care system if Chloe ended up winning the battle and killing me. And then the thought of the state finding the last family member left, Chloe, and giving her physical custody made me sick.

Nauseous.

"I'm going to ask you one more time. Where are those kids?"

I stood my ground and remained defiant, as she walked up to me close enough for me to smell the scent of sex and death that rested on her skin. She raised the bottle and smiled. "Fine, have it your way. Open wide…"

Chapter Twenty-Four

(Chloe)

Driving crazy.
Adrenaline pumping.
Hoping to kill within minutes.

I pushed aside any concern I had for the police, while
dodging in and out of traffic. I had already made it past
Broadway, and was racing down State Street. Feeling like
my future was on the line, I thought long and hard about how
I would handle things when I got to the hotel. Bella, of
course, would be killed. There were no other options. She
had ruined my life for the last two years and needed to be
taken out. Mye, I wasn't sure…his fate had possibilities. I
could just shoot him…two blanks to the head…or maybe
even take him to his mother and kill them both together.

Before I could even bring myself to focus on Oshyn's
date with death, my phone rang. It was a Raleigh area code,
yet the number didn't ring a bell for me. I wondered who
would be calling me at a time like this. As I turned the corner
sharply, I answered with bass in my voice.

"Yeah," I spat.

The voice was frail and weak and unrecognizable, as
the person spoke softly into the phone.

"Tommy, is that you?" I was clearly irritated.

181

"Chloe, I...I...I...I...n...e...e...e...e...d to see you," he struggled to say.   "Tommy, I gotta call you back later. I'm handling something right now." The tone in my voice should've been a sign that I couldn't talk, but he insisted.

"Chloe, there may not be a later," he informed sadly. "You gotta sign one more paper that I forgot about."

A lump formed in my throat and I instantly got wet. Visions invaded my head of me in all black, big wide hat, and tons of people giving me their condolences. Most of all, I had his money. All of it.

"Chloe, do you hear me?" Tommy asked in his fragile voice. "The lawyer said it has to be signed."

"Yeah, I hear you. I'll fly out tomorrow."

"No, Chloe," he pleaded. "The latest...the latest, the latest," he kept saying.

I became irritated. "The latest what?"

"The latest is now...it's very bad. I could go at any time," He struggled to get his words out clearly. "The doc said things don't look so good. I've taken a turn for the worse."

"A turn for the worse?" I questioned, as a mini grin slipped through the side of my lips.

"This is the best I've felt all day. But who knows."

Tommy began to cry like a bitch. A weak man on his death bed was always beyond pitiful, but I listened anyway as I took the exit ramp, planning to make a u-turn to head to the airport. He kept talking while I made plans to get to Raleigh to sign the necessary paper. It would be well worth it in the end, I convinced myself.

Four hours, thirty-three minutes later, I had landed in the land of prosperity.
Raleigh, North Carolina.

A place where I used to get money.

182

A place full of memories.

Both good and bad.

My heels clicked along the cold floor as I pranced my way down the halls of Wake Med Hospital. As usual, all eyes were focused on me. I was tired from the plane ride, but it didn't affect my appearance much. I had stopped in the bathroom on the first floor so I could freshen up and spread some gloss on my lips for Tommy. I wanted to look good as I signed my name on the dotted line. When I got to his room, I pushed on the closed door slowly, unsure of what I would see.

The stench.

That awful hospital smell.

It all hit me as soon as the door opened. Luckily Tommy had a spacious room, so as soon I walked in and closed the door, I had already scoped out the place, trying to see where I would sleep. He had a single room, no roommate, so I wondered who the two extra people were who chatted over in the corner with the nurse in the Pooh Bear scrubs. They talked intensely, using library voices, while staring me down in the process. One woman left abruptly, but not before I shot her the evilest expression I could muster. I wasn't sure if the other lady in all white was a social worker, or from the department who handles people who were about to die. I was hoping for the later, considering Tommy looked like shit on a stick.

Without hesitation, I flew over to Tommy's bed, sat by his side, and threw my head, like a drama queen, onto his torso. I just knew he would be glad to see me. Oddly, his body didn't move. Seemed that he had no reflexes. No movement at all. At first my thought was that he'd passed already until I felt his stomach inflating and deflating slowly. He was still alive, yet it was clear Tommy wouldn't make it much longer.

It dawned on me that I had arrived just in time. I could've kicked myself in the ass for not watching over my jackpot more closely. By his side was where I should've been for days, instead of fooling with Oshyn and Carlos. I sat back in the chair trying to get comfortable, then grabbed a notice-able business magazine sitting on the small table next to his bed. Today's Entrepreneur, it read. I grabbed it, noticing Tommy was featured on the cover. The tag line read, One Man's Journey to Millions in the Stock Market. *Damn, Tommy looked decent on the cover*, I told myself, slipping the magazine into my purse to read later. *I should've played him more closely, I thought. Would probably be sitting extra pretty by now.*

The more I thought about my mistakes, the more I felt someone's presence watching me. From the corner of my eye I noticed the same woman in white moving curiously in my direction. Everything was quiet, until she had the audac-ity to ask me who I was.

"I'm his soul mate," I blasted. "He called so I came as fast as I could," I informed, while forcing water to well up in my eyes. It was hard, but I had to think of anything that would make me cry. And so I did. It was my life. That fact that I could never find love. The fact that every person I ever met fucked me over. I started thinking about myself, selfishly, just as I always did when other people needed me.

I sort of tuned the woman out until she said, "I'm Ms. Stevens."

My eyes grew two times their normal size. The bitch had actually called out Tommy's last name. It was possible that she was a younger sister, perhaps even a cousin. Cer-tainly not a secret wife that he had not told me about. Imme-diately, I started to drill her with questions.

"So what relation are you?"

"No, tell me more about you," she countered.

"Look, you some long lost cousin," I began to say, but the sounding of the machines going off startled us both.

We both turned our attention back to Tommy, with the emotional woman rushing to the opposite side of his bed. She was a skinny, tall woman shaped like a model with no ass at all. She wasn't too cute if you asked me, especially with the freckle thing going on all over the middle of her face.

We both took turns rubbing his arms, and trying to get him to respond to us. I needed him to be coherent so I could ask for the last paper that I had to sign. But his eyes were still glossy and half-closed, as I said, "Tommy, I'm here, baby. You told me to come, so I came. Where's the paper, baby?"

The nurse looked at me crazily, and asked me to step back for a second. I obliged for seconds, until she said, "His heart rate is getting even lower. Not good."

My facial gestures showed my confusion, but it seemed the nurse and the woman knew more than I did. They were obviously in tune with one another. It was clear by the way they exchanged saddened looks, followed by deep eye contact. I just turned my attention to Tommy, who continued to lay all the way back, almost stiff like a mummy and appearing almost incoherent. It seemed like he was waiting on death to touch him on the shoulder. His breathing had been irregular every since I entered the room, but was now becoming more sluggish. When I saw his eyes rolling up into his head, I touched his hand, which felt colder than ice, then made myself drop a tear.

"Tommy, I really need that paper," I whispered into his ear. "It's me, baby, I'm here," I told him, hoping for some sign.

"Rest easy, I'm here," the mysterious woman said, obviously competing with me. She began patting his forehead, trying to make his journey a comforting one. Me, I was in a state of panic. I needed to sign on the dotted line, and Tommy was two steps from death. I didn't give a fuck about how he left the earth...comfy or not. I just wanted my inheritance.

"Oh Tommy," I called out. "Don't leave me, Tommy! We've been through so much together," I moaned loudly, then grabbed his hand again. "Wake up, Tommy, wake up!"

Suddenly, Tommy opened his eyes slightly, then mouthed a few shocking words. "Chloe, you deceived me

185

sweetie."

I got up close in his face, and rubbed his arm letting him know I was by his side. "Rest easy, don't strain yourself."

"N-o-o-o-o, I got-t-t-t-a tell you. I know the investigators came through," he confessed in a light whisper. "No daughter, no love for me…"

"Shhhhh," I said in a caring tone hoping he would shut the fuck up. I swallowed hard wondering what he meant. "But you called me honey, I'm here. Don't worry yourself about anything else."

"Yeah…I called," he said, almost with a smirk. "I needed you to know that I know…" It seemed he was on *some get back,* but I wasn't sure. The sickness had him beat so he couldn't even finish his sentence.

Then it happened.

My demise began.

The bitch flew from the opposite side of the bed and touched me on the shoulder. "No disrespect, Miss, but you really have to go."

"And who's going to make me," I replied. I stood up, ready to buck.

"Me. I'm the next of kin," she told me firmly. "I'm his daughter, and I don't think that you're supposed to be here."

I turned my neck slowly like the crazy bitch from the *The Exorcist.*

"What did you say to me? I'm Chloe Rodriquez, his woman!" I pointed at Tommy, like I wanted a dying man to back me up.

"Listen, my father is dying. They expected him to be gone by now." Her voice was confrontational. "This is a private moment for us, so I'd like for you to leave us to I can say goodbye properly."

"Look," I said boldly, "I'm his beneficiary, so I should be able to say goodbye too." I made sure to sound like I really cared. "I signed papers just days ago, so I should be able to stay just like you." I swung my eyes over to the nurse for approval.

"Listen, my father and his lawyer had those papers re-scinded. I signed the new paperwork. So go," she insisted, shooing me off like a fly. "You'll never touch my father's money. Besides, he doesn't even know you. You took advantage of his illness, and he wasn't in his right mind when it happened. You won't be an Anna Nicole to my family," she added coldly.

"That's n...o....t t...r...u...e," I stuttered. "He called me."

A huge smile erupted on her face when she let out her neck words. "Those papers were torn to shreds. He called me right after he talked to you. Too late," she teased.

My mind was being fucked with.

Picked at.

Torn apart.

I thought Tommy had everything covered, I wondered to myself. *Weren't the papers I signed worth anything? Wasn't there something someone could do?* My mental state had been descending for several minutes, and Tommy's daughter knew it. It could've been the smoke blowing through my nose, or the fire in my eyes that warned her. Suddenly, I exploded.

I sprang from my space then leaped across the room in search of Tommy's personal belongings. And in a voice not altogether steady, said, "I signed papers less than three days ago."

I got no response, so I started throwing shit that he had stored in the bottom of his closet. There were all old photos of him and his daughter, mostly from her toddler days. Before I finished they were all scattered across the floor, and I moved to the two drawers next to his bed. Both his daughter and the nurse paid my rampage no mind, because while I tore the room apart, Tommy had taken his last breath.

"He's gone," the nurse said sympathetically. She acted as though I didn't exist, as I rubbed up against her slightly, still pulling shit out the drawers.

Tommy's daughter, on the other hand, showed her dislike for me differently. She pulled the white sheet quickly over her father's body all the way up to his eyes, as if she didn't want his dead spirit to witness her next move. She then lifted the phone and asked for Security.

I started shouting, "You think that shit scares me! All I want is my money! Tommy promised me an inheritance and I want it!"

She kept looking at me crazily, while moving closer to her father's bed. It was almost as if she were protecting him. "Did you ever love my father?" she asked me.

"What a stupid fucking question. Where's the paper?" I asked again.

She wouldn't answer. Simply smiled her victory. My instinct told me not to back down, but the two uniformed visitors at the door told me firmly that it was time to go.

Chapter Twenty-Five
(Oshyn)

She spared me.
Maybe she loved me.
For real.

I wanted to think that for once in my life she had left without inflicting any more pain on me, but I knew better. The acid that she had intended to pour down my throat would have killed me instantly, but that wasn't what she wanted. Before leaving to go and find the kids, Chloe changed her mind at the very last minute. The deadly liquid would have dissolved my teeth, ate up the lining of my throat and esophagus, and it would have made the blood that flowed freely through my body boil, like it had done the water. But she didn't want me to die just then.

I knew that the reason was because she wanted to watch us all suffer and cry out in agony while she sat and witnessed. She had no intention this time of fucking up and letting us slip away, but somewhere along the way she had made a terrible mistake. She had underestimated my determination to live. My determination to save my family, as well as my determination to wipe her off the face of this earth. I wanted her dead just as much as she wanted me dead, and now once again, I had my chance.

With the ropes already loosened, and flesh that was already raw, I continued to work effortlessly to get myself free and get to my kids before Chloe had a chance to. I was well aware of the big head start that she had already gained on me, but I was confident that my grandmother would somehow mess up Chloe's plans. She promised me that she would keep them safe, and I knew that she would keep her word.

I managed to wrestle and slide the rough rope from my burning skin and worked quickly to untie the same rope that held my ankles hostage. Now the ropes that were once used to bind my hands and feet together lay unraveled on the floor, and as soon as I went to stand up, my legs gave out and I fell to the floor. I was weak, exhausted and hungry. *Get up!* I said to myself, as I used the concrete floor as a mattress, but I just couldn't bear to move. The only ounce of energy I had left was used to set myself free, and now I had nothing left to give. My breaths had quickly become like a fish out of water.

Short.

Fast.

Numbered.

I closed my eyes, wanting nothing more other than to sleep all of this pain away, and wake up to find that this had all been just a really bad nightmare, but I knew that I wouldn't be so lucky. This was as real as it got, and there was no amount of wishful thinking that would have gotten me out of this mess I was in. This was my life, plain and simple.

The blackness I saw because of my closed eyes had now been replaced with the images of Bella and Mye playing together and loving each other. Then my visions switched to images of Chloe torturing them, blood everywhere, and them reaching out to me in fear, and when their screams came to a ceasing halt and their eyes closed, indicating that they were beginning their journey to the other side, that's when mine opened.

Get the fuck up! I said to myself once more, actually listening this time. At an injured turtle's pace, I slowly lifted myself up and stood to my feet. I managed to begin walking to the door, and with each step I took, gained a little bit of strength along the way. I got out of the warehouse and to my car. After digging into my pocket to retrieve my keys, I unlocked my door, jumped in and started it. I looked down at myself, and realized how much blood I had on me. So much that I was soaking in it. Just by the little movement I made in the car, it was starting to look like a crime scene too so I pulled off, knowing that I had to drive carefully back to the hotel in order to avoid being pulled over by the police.

I had a feeling that Mye and Bella were still in the hotel room, and that my grandmother was still keeping them out of harm's way like she had promised. My hands began to tremble uncontrollably as the thought of me walking into the room and seeing them chopped up into a million pieces crept into my mind. One thing Chloe never did was make idle threats, and always carried out what she said she would do, so I couldn't help but to think that she had kept her word.

"Ju must hurry up and get back to the hotel. The kids are in great danger if ju don't make it there soon!"

Thinking that I was alone in the car, I turned to my right and saw my grandmother sitting beside me, looking at me with a chilling stare.

"Why aren't you with them?" I asked, horrified at the fact that she was sitting here with me instead of where she was supposed to be.

"Ju were supposed to get rid of her!" she blurted out, ignoring my question. "This is jur fault! Ju let her get away, and now she's going to kill them!"

Kill them…kill them…kill them, were the words that floated around in my head, as her aged voice continued to echo in my mind. Her mouth continued to move as inaudible broken English sentences flew out of her mouth at a mile a minute, but I couldn't hear anything anymore. I just drove straight, as the words "kill them" made a permanent resi-

191

dence in my heart.

I drove the car, not really paying any attention to the road, and was scared shitless back to reality by a host of honking horns. I had run a red light and almost caused a massive accident, but I didn't care. I would have run it anyway, even if I had of seen it because I needed to get to them. I was just glad that there were no police around.

My driving mimicked a drunk driver, as I recklessly weaved in and out of traffic, no longer able to assume responsibility for my actions. I had become intoxicated with death. My pores and breath reeked of it. Still in a daze, I drove up on the beginning of a huge cemetery. With Mama still in my passenger seat rambling on, I turned to my left and watched the tombstones breeze by me. I couldn't help but to wonder if this is where they laid Brooklyn to rest, or if they would cremate his body because it was cheaper and there was no one to claim him.

Couldn't help but to wonder if his spirit would come and talk to me as my grandmother and first born son, Micah's, did. I couldn't help but to hope and wonder if God would appoint my husband as my guardian angel. I prayed that he would so that I could feel his presence on my life just one more time. The graveyard that I couldn't seem to pry from my eyes had now become his home, and I couldn't find it in my heart to be okay with that.

As visions of a future without my husband began haunting me, the words *kill them…kill them* somehow seemed to have crept back in, followed by a tremendously loud bang, and my chest being rammed into the steering wheel. The airbag that had burst into my face had just as quickly deflated. I saw that I had run into the back of a police car.

Hard.

The hood of my car was now curled up and his rear was banged in. I had realized that he had been sitting at a red light when I banged into him, and watched intensely as he jumped out of his car.

"Ma'am, get out of the car!" he yelled harshly, obviously pissed that I had ruined his day.

"Mama! Mama!" I screamed frantically, as I looked in the passenger seat where she once sat. "Where is my grandmother?"

The balding white officer peered into my car, in an attempt to look for an injured woman, but found nothing.

"Ma'am, you're the only person in here."

"No, we *have* to find her. She was just here, talking to me and I wasn't listening. She was trying to tell me something and I stopped listening and now she's gone!" I took a look at him, and noticed him slowly putting his hand on his gun.

"Where did all of that blood come from? Are you hurt?" The tone of suspicion was heavy in his voice, as he realized that this was more than a reckless driving charge. I held on to the steering wheel, and with every suffocating breath I took, I could feel the bruise that began to develop on my breasts. The tears began to fly out of my eyes.

My panic started to attack.

"Where are you bleeding from?"

"My children!" I hollered. "I have to get to my children! I have to save them!" I did what I could to move the airbag out of my face, and tried putting the car in reverse until I realized that it had been cut off.

"Get out of the car now!" he demanded, after opening my door.

"But you don't understand. She's going to kill them," I confessed. But I quickly learned that my cries were falling on deaf ears, just as my grandmother's had to mine just moments before.

The street wasn't busy, but a few travelers that frequented the lane we now stopped up, had to find alternate routes to their destination. I had inconvenienced them. I had inconvenienced me.

"The state will take your kids," he threatened. "Did you hear me? You will lose them, and custody will be awarded to

193

the state or next of kin." He paused. Waited for a response. "That's it. I'm going to take you in."

As the officer's thick build stepped forward to physically take me out of the car, I reacted quickly by slamming my door shut and attempting to turn the car on one more time. This time the ignition rumbled as my vehicle decided to finally go along with my plans. I threw the gear in reverse, forcing him to jump out of the way as my car released itself off of his. Although the appearance of it was bad, it still ran good enough to get me to my destination.

"Stop now!" he demanded, as he ran in front of the car with his gun drawn and pointed it at me. "Stop or I'll shoot," he warned.

But I couldn't stop.

It was either me or him, and I refused to be taken into custody. I refused to lose this battle. I threw the gear into drive, and before another threat had a chance to fly out of his mouth, I hit the gas, slamming him in between my car and his. Threats no longer came out of his mouth. Just screams that said he would be on desk duty for the rest of his life.

Stuck in my own world, I snapped out of my daze and back into reality, as I realized that a few bystanders had witnessed me paralyzing a uniformed police officer. I knew I had to make moves quickly. With him lying on the hood of my car, I put it in reverse again and pushed the gas until he slid onto the ground. People began to rush to his aid and sirens rang in the distant background, as I put the weapon that I now drove back into drive and made my way back onto the main street in the direction of the hotel before it was too late.

Chapter Twenty-Six
(Chloe)

As soon as the plane landed back on New York soil, I hopped up from my seat, barging my way to the front. People stared, pointed, and even called me names. Surely, I didn't give a fuck! A tyrant was what I had become as I pushed them all out of my way, cursing them as I left them behind. Some complained loudly as I stepped across luggage bags, laptop bags, and even strollers that found themselves in my way. I was a bitch on a mission, ready to do some serious damage.

The entire flight back to Rochester had become a nightmare for me. My head hurt like hell, as thoughts bounced through my mind. All I could think about was how I had lost out on Tommy's inheritance. My only chance at getting lump sums of money without relying on a nigga.

"His bitch-ass daughter would pay," I told myself under my breath, while waiting for the cabin door to open. It was crazy how I took a chance on leaving Oshyn alone and had even abandoned the idea of kidnapping Bella and Mye, all in an effort to become a Millionaire Mistress again. All for nothing!" I shouted furiously.

The head stewardess shot me a funny look, as I

195

brushed myself up against some old woman that I had pushed out of the aisle and back into her seat. I wanted it to be clear that I would be the first one out the door. Had places to go, people to see. "Turn your head, bitch!" I blasted the young stewardess.

She was about to say something back. But just as my hand cupped, ready to pimp slap her, the door opened, and like I planned, I filed out first, cutting off the woman with the small baby in front of me. Like a power walker on a mission, I jetted down the gangway, hoping to quickly get to my rental, which was parked in the daily parking lot. My walk was brisk as I ran every person down who appeared in my path.

I had almost made it to the end of the concourse, when a flat screen hanging above an open bar area caught my attention. My skin oozed with joy when I saw his face. It was Carlos, dead and center on Channel 11 ten o'clock news. It read, CAPTURED, yet I couldn't make out the words spoken by the newscaster. The television's volume was rather low, and the white folks that sat around the bar were too loud. I started to tell them all to shut the fuck up, but wanted to relish in the delight of seeing Carlos busted. "That nigga got what he deserved," I chanted under my breath. I started laughing loudly, almost in a crazy-like state. People began to stare at me, but I didn't care.

I smiled broadly while reaching into my purse in search of an Advil. *I would take three*, I told myself, as my fingers touched the bottle. Just as I pulled the bottle from my purse, my eyes refocused on the second picture that had been added to the screen.

It was a mug shot.

My mug shot.

I was now a fugitive.

Anger filled my insides as I shouted out, "Shit!"

I banged against the granite countertop on the bar, saying, "Fuck, fuck, fuck!" But my words were cut short by several fingers pointing my way. Rudely, I eyed the muthu-fuckas ferociously, ready to step to anybody who thought they should be involved in my business. One woman looked at the screen, then at me, then back at the screen again. And just like the perfect citizen, one older white man close to his eighties had a nerve to hop up and rush over to a security guard.

With nerve, I stood in place, while the older man pointed to me, then back to the TV. As he was giving his side of the story, the guard got on his walkie-talkie and called in the militia. I finally figured out I needed to move when I saw two uniformed guards walking briskly from the other end. Within seconds, I darted down the hallway, then took the escalators toward baggage claim. I wasn't far from the entrance, but could see airport security getting thicker around the outside exit and entrance areas. I had to think fast.

My eyes spotted a few unattended luggage bags off to the side. Some flowery prints, others extra ugly. But one caught my attention. It was a plain black roll bag with a huge hat sitting on top near the handle. Of course I snatched it, hoping the owner wouldn't see me and cause a scene. Before I knew it, I had reached into my purse, slipped on my shades, headed out the door, and pulled the large brim hat as close down on my face as possible.

Outside, I jetted across the parking lot, realizing the weather was changing in Rochester. It was windy, and starting to get much cooler in the evenings. The darkness was perfect, making it harder to make out my disguise, but the wind kept hitting me in the face.

After making it to the car, my heart rate settled a bit. I dove into the front seat and backed out the space doing thirty miles an hour. The police were already after me, so of course I barged through the yellow gate where I was supposed to pay a fee. *Fuck rules*, I told myself. I was ready to go hard again, getting back to what I knew best.

It didn't take long before I had taken curve after curve, and made it off the airport grounds safely, but now had to make myself unnoticeable while I grabbed the children from the hotel. I was sure by now everyone had seen my face splattered across their television screen. Yet I had to make things work.

Everything was happening so fast I could barely think straight. I knew I had to get to the hotel, so I took the downtown exit headed that way. Still in all, I worried about Oshyn. I hoped she was still alive so that I would have the opportunity to kill her myself. I wanted to live with the memory of being the person who took her life. Her and her kids.

Just then it hit me. My plan was coming together. Once at the hotel, I would kidnap the kids, put them in my trunk, and take them both to die with their mother. It would be sweet. A family that dies together, how nice the sound, I laughed.

Just as more crazy thoughts and anger filled my bones, flashing lights ahead made my heart stop momentarily. Sweat beaded against my forehead, and my wide brim hat began to itch my face. The six visible police cars and the five car back up confirmed that my assumption was right. It was a road block. One I would have to pass.

"Fuck!" I shouted, thrusting my head down and banging it against the steering wheel.

I was now the fourth car in line, and breathing like an asthmatic. Fear filled my senses, as I contemplated what I would say. It became clear that they were asking for identification by the way the officer talked nicely to the woman three cars ahead of me, as she handed him something from her window. My guess…a driver's license.

"What fucking luck," I told myself, while holding the wheel tightly like my life depended on it. "A fugitive and a road block!"

Within seconds, we had moved up again, making me third in line. My heart beat even faster, and I had decided to act as though my license had been lost once I got up to the officer in charge. I pumped myself up, believing everything would be okay, as I watched three officers rearing back on the hood of one of the cruisers. They laughed and grinned as if they didn't have a care in the world. So my senses told me the roadblock had nothing to do with me. I had gotten side-tracked for moments after looking at the other officer's mannerisms. My nosiness had cost me though. Before I knew it, the man in front of me was asked to remove himself from the car.

Instantly, I panicked, backed up like a race car driver, and smashed into the white Camry behind me. It didn't take long before two of the laughing officers finally noticed me. Moments later, I had made a u-turn after struggling to maneuver the steering wheel quickly enough. Before I knew it, I was racing down the wrong side of the road, with two police cars and blaring sirens behind me.

It was like a scene from the movie, *Set It Off* where Queen Latifah refused to give in. I knew I wouldn't pull over. It wasn't my time for jail.

Had children to kidnap.

People to kill.

My destiny wasn't over.

Chapter Twenty-Seven
(Chloe)

"Hello, my name is Oshyn Rodriquez," I said calmly, with a plastic smile spread across my face. "I misplaced my room key, can I get another?"

My hands were folded neatly across one another as I leaned my body over the counter. I kept my smile going as the woman punched a few keys on the computer.

"What room number is that? I don't see Oshyn Rodriquez," the woman said.

Shit! I punched myself in the forehead for forgetting that Oshyn was married. "I mean Oshyn Jones," I corrected.

The woman looked at me strangely then typed some more. I could tell she was going to be a problem from the way she refused to give me eye contact. She was a hater; a big-boned bitch who hated shapely women, but who shocked me with her next comment.

"Can I see some identification?"

"Look-a-here, Michelle," I said, eyeing her nametag, "I've had a long day. I lost my purse, and then to top it off, got pulled over by the cops." My voice started trembling as I switched into actress mode. "And…and…and…my daughter is sick, I mean really ill, and her father left me!" I started crying, tears dripping on the front desk, the whole nine. It went on for minutes until I finally looked up to see Michelle's expression.

It was blank.

She wasn't feeling me.

At all.

Within seconds, I sniffed my fake snot back up into my nostrils, and put my game face on. I knew nothing in life was free, so I pulled a twenty from my back pocket and laid it near her fingertips. From the looks of things, the chick shopped at T.J. Max so a twenty was perfect. My first impulse was to reach over the counter, and yank the bitch by the neck. But I chilled. I exhaled a few times then spoke through my clutched teeth. "I need the key to my room please."

"Miss, I'll need to see some identification," she repeated, throwing the twenty back across the counter.

I got angry, reached across the counter, and turned the black computer in my direction. "Cut the key," I told her in a fury.

She looked to her left, like she was signaling back-up. Little did she know, the name Brooklyn Jones, Room 254 was clearly exposed on the screen. Without delay, I slid back off my tiptoes and apologized mildly.

"Look, I've had a bad day. Forget about the key," I said politely. "I'll just wait over there for my husband." I grinned.

Michelle walked to the back without even saying another word. Maybe she was going to snitch after all. I didn't care. It was about me and my mission. While I had the chance, I sped around the corner and dipped inside the breakfast area until Michelle was back in sight. She talked about me for sure to another male employee who showed up as back-up. At one point they turned away, giving me my chance. I moved like an agent on a mission, making my way toward the stairwell. As soon as the coast was clear, I darted beneath the exit sign, opened the stairwell door, and ran up the staircase, headed to end the Jones name once and for all.

Taking two steps at a time, I wondered how I would get into the room. Bella was smart for her age, so letting me in was a no-no. I would have to be creative, sneaky, and pry my way in if necessary. Someone seeing me posed a big problem. The hotel wasn't packed at all, but nothing was ever safe when it came to killing.

When I reached the second floor, the feeling shook me a bit. It was sorta eerie and deserted, almost like nobody moved about frequently. I guess that was a good thing, so they wouldn't hear Bella scream. I didn't trust the bitch, Michelle, from the front. She might've been on a mission to check the floor, just to see if I had doubled back. Then again, she didn't appear to be that smart.

Once on the floor, I moved slowly, checking for even numbers. Room 254 was just five doors down from the stairwell, and a sight for sore eyes. I wasted no time, boom, boom, boom! I banged on the door like the fuckin' police.

"Bella, open the door, it's Auntie." I laughed, then grabbed my stomach abruptly. I had been hit with a sudden pain, one deep inside my gut. "C'mon out Bella!" I yelled. "You not getting outta here alive," I sang.

Still nothing.

So I kicked the damn door.

"Bella, do you fuckin' hear me!"

I kicked it again, again and again, before stepping back. I decided to walk away as if I were leaving. *Maybe she would be dumb enough to think I left then open up*, I told myself. Just like that my feet treaded slowly moving backwards pass Rooms 252, 250 and 248. Suddenly I stopped.

"Chloe!" someone called out.

"Oh shit!" *Someone called my name*. The voice I knew so well.

I turned around, exposing my victory grin when I saw her. I wanted to make her think I had already succeeded, beat her to the kids. Oshyn looked tired, worn, her hair in disarray. Probably needed a bath. She reminded me of Jason from *Friday the 13th*…never wanting to die. *How the fuck did she get loose?* I asked myself.

"What did you do to my kids, Chloe?" She gritted her teeth and balled her fist in anger. Maybe her fiery stare was supposed to scare me. Maybe she wanted me to scream. Maybe the tone in her voice scared others, but not me.

Once again the pain hit me hard. A pain that damn near knocked me off my feet, but I stood up straight and stepped a few more feet away from the door. "Oh, we had a great time. I just left them inside," I teased. "They've gone to hell now," I boasted. "You'll see them both soon, bloody and all."

"Nooooooo Chloe! Tell me you didn't!" she cried out, hurling her head into her hands.

I clutched my stomach, barley able to make it down the hallway back in Oshyn's direction. It was a must that she died, and something I wanted to confess. But the intense cramping kept getting worse as I walked toward her, and she toward me. Just that fast it started to feel like my intestines were being tied into small tiny knots, but I kept talking shit.

"This is it, Oshyn. Your crazy ass gotta go." I wasn't sure how I would kill her, but I knew I would. She was coming at me full force with confidence, and for some strange reason, I thought with a weapon in her hand. I stumbled, almost needing a cane, yet continued to walk her way. Before I could say something slick, I threw up. It was a smell that instantly stunk up the hallway, causing me to want to vomit again. Oshyn shrieked at the smell, stopping her in her tracks. Then out of nowhere, shit got worse. I became hot, body like a furnace, and cheeks red like fire. Reality hit, and I was all of a sudden afraid of Oshyn.

Just four feet away she exposed the small blade, letting me know she was serious. For the first time in my life, Oshyn now had me afraid. I was so nauseous, I wasn't sure I could fight back.

Before I knew it, she had swung her foot around like

she was on some Bruce Lee shit, and kicked me straight in the middle of my forehead. Instantly, I fell to the ground like a rag doll, then was immediately hit in the mouth with a powerful punch. Everything was happening so fast, I was unable to think, so I lay still, unsure if I could even move. Then from the corner of my eye, I spotted a young man opening his door, peeping to see what all the commotion was about. I bellowed for help, but just like most black people, he wasn't trying to help. Within seconds he disappeared, and no one else came into view.

Vivid pictures of the gypsy's wrinkled face invaded my mind, as I struggled to forget the red dust she'd blown in my face. Red dust that carried promises of wealth, true love, and revenge at the hands of another. So far, none of her predictions had come true. But the revenge piece now had possibilities.

Oshyn had begun throwing quick, powerful haymakers my way, proving that she had lost her mind. She hit me like Tyson banged out his opponents who never had the opportunity to fight back. She was whipping my ass, and there was nothing I could do about it. I was balled up in a knot, and could only feel the whipping she was putting on my face and body. My vision had become blurry, and only the gypsy's face flashed before me as my body got weaker by the minute. My skin began to crawl with imaginary insects that I couldn't see or kill. I just laid on the floor, attempting to shield my head from my sister's vicious blows.

Nothing worked.

I just couldn't fight off the brutal beating.

"My children! Where are they, and what the fuck have you done with them!" Oshyn shouted, as she hovered over me, desperately hoping for an answer.

I couldn't speak, barely could see. All I wanted was a doctor or someone to help me. It wasn't just the pain from Oshyn's defeat. My agony also stemmed from some sort of unexplainable illness taking place in my body. Although it felt like an alien had entered my body, blood dripped down the top of my head as I tried to raise my head to talk to Oshyn.

Instead, I laughed when I looked at her face. "Haha-hahahahah, you stupid bitch." She snatched me by my neck like a rag doll. "Where are they?" she asked again, and followed it up immediately with another blow to my face. This time with her fist, followed by a swipe across the forehead with the knife.

I stretched my jaw out in pain just about the same time that I let out an agonizing sound. "Ahhhhhhhhh shit!" I wondered where she had gotten her energy from. I had tortured her days before, and stole her hope, yet she seemed invincible, and stronger than before.

"Where are they, Chloe?" she said, throwing another hard punch to my left jaw.

"Those muthafuckers are dead," I struggled to say, then smiled, showing all the blood that had now stained my teeth and gums. "I chopped those bastards into pieces. Very…small…pieces," I told her, loosing more energy.

I expected her to cry just like she did when she lost her first son. But she didn't. Strangely, the bitch grinned satanically, and portrayed a sudden calmness. Oshyn pulled her right hand from her side, stared at the knife, and before I got a chance to say anything else, stabbed me in the abdomen.

"You…you…you…fucking…bitch…bitch!' I said in between my small, painful breaths. It was clear I now looked like a fish out of water, gulping for air. Praying for life. "You…you…st…ab…ed me? *You* stabbed *me!*" I cried, wanting my voice to have the ability to get louder.

I was dumbfounded.

Losing my fight.

Beat by Oshyn?

It wasn't supposed to end like this. She wasn't supposed to escape and grow some balls. *I was supposed to win*, I kept telling myself. I kept thinking about her weaknesses, as she rammed the knife into my chest and stomach multiple times and kept it there as my life poured all over her.

She had become a monster, someone I didn't know any-more. And as crazy as it sounded, my blood was now on her hands. All of it. All five pints that soiled my clothes and the carpet along the floor. And my death would soon follow.

"I loved you," Oshyn confessed, as she dropped the weapon and stepped over me slowly. She cried like a punk, while her chest heaved up and down quickly. She wanted to say more, but I knew she wanted to get to the room to check on her kids. I wanted to think about how I would've killed Bella if I had gotten in the room, but my eyes had begun their decent toward the back of my head, while my body temperature dropped drastically. I was cold, incoherent, but still heard Oshyn's soft tone repeating, "I loved you."

She repeated more words as the tears streamed down her face, and she banged on her hotel door. Her fist beat rapidly and vigorously, as she shouted her children's names.

"Bella, Mye," she screamed.

I knew she was probably still screaming, but I could no longer hear her. The floor had speedily become bombarded with employees and hotel guest rambling about in a panic asking, "What happened!"

They were frantic as one woman kneeled to help me, and another rushed to catch Oshyn, when an employee opened the door and announced that the room was empty.

I saw her mouth motion the words, "Where are my fucking kids!" just before her body dropped. *Weak bitch*, I thought.

If only I had the energy to laugh.

The ability to tease.

The strength to take credit for their absence.

But I couldn't. I couldn't feel nothing anymore. Couldn't taste nothing either. And could no longer see. My vision of Oshyn laid back in someone's arms faded, and was replaced with the gypsy's. I was sure my spirit was slipping into death as the old woman smiled at me. Her lips were still crusty as she spoke evil words.

Familiar words.
Words that had come true.
You will die… and burn in hell forever.
Within seconds everything was black.

Chapter Twenty-Eight
(Oshyn)

"Bella!" I yelled. "Bella!"

I burst into the room after regaining consciousness. The bathroom was first, then I checked under the beds and looked in the closet, right before peeking out onto the patio. I didn't see anyone. Mye's bottles lay empty on the floor and the bed was tussled and undone.

"Bella, where are you!"

My cries fell to no one.

I flopped on the bed and buried my face into the messy white sheets, smearing Chloe's blood everywhere, while trying to cry my pain away. *Where could they be?* I asked myself, too emotionally and physically drained to actually come up with the answer. *Maybe Chloe was telling the truth*, I thought, as more images of their little limbs being torn from their bodies filled my mind.

"Ju did good," a familiar voice behind me said. I popped my head up and spun around only to see my grandmother standing in front of me alone. "I am so proud of ju. Chloe was evil like her mother and a shame to our family. What ju did needed to be done," she assured me.

"Where are the kids?" I asked her.

"But this time she won't come back!" she said, totally ignoring my question. "Ju got rid of her for good. She's gone forever. Ju did good, my child."

"But where is Mye and Bella?"

"Now it's up to ju to build this family back up again. A strong bloodline of strong children."

"Why are you ignoring me?" I asked as I went to touch her shoulder, but my hand went right through her. I saw her but she wasn't there. "Mama, please don't do this to me!" I screamed, but she just continued to talk over me. As if she wasn't responsible for the kids. As if I hadn't left them in her care. As if she didn't know who they were. "Don't do this to me!" I repeated one last time before the room began to spin.

"It's time for me to go, but I will always be in your presence. Watching over ju."

"But you were supposed to be watching over the kids!" I reminded her. "Where are they? Just don't leave! Please, tell me something before you go!"

She smiled and just simply repeated, "I will always be in your presence." And with that she was gone without a trace.

"Nooooo!" I yelled out in agony, but it was too late. I had been abandoned yet again. Feeling my knees getting ready to go out, I quickly sought refuge on the bed, where I laid down and curled up into a fetal position.

The room continued to spin, as I tried coming to terms with Brooklyn and the kids being taken, but no amount of rocking could soothe the pain of loss I had in my chest. My heart no longer existed. In its place lay a shadow of darkness that was incapable of loving again. Not able to take the pain anymore, I took the bloody knife out of my pocket, and for a moment just held it in my hand.

Chloe's blood soiled and stained the sheets I laid on, and now I was contemplating letting my own blood do the same. I would never feel his warm body and soft lips touch me again, and I would never hear the laughter of my baby or see Bella's green eyes look at me like a daughter would her mother. I was left on this earth to fend for myself, and I had made the decision to move on.

I held my left hand out and ran the razor sharp blade across my wrists the long way. I wanted my life to slip away quickly so I could join everybody sooner. The blood gushed out of my veins as I felt my body getting weaker and weaker, as my soul drifted away. A smile managed to make its way on my face, and I closed my eyes to get ready for my journey to the light. Life as I knew it seemed to get a little colder.

My breathing slowed down.

Drastically.

And then it stopped.

Chapter Twenty-Nine
(Chloe)

Three weeks later

Miserable.

Still sick on the stomach.

And now frustrated.

It had been three weeks since my altercation with Oshyn, and only one week since my release from Highland Hospital. Oshyn did me in with her punk ass stabbing, but I got fixed. Crazy thing is that I still felt that shit deep inside. My body lacked oomph, and my stomach was beyond damaged.

Finally, I gathered enough energy to drag myself into this whack-ass doctor's office, where I now sat in the tiny waiting room, waiting. I'd decided to pull the Today's Entrepreneur magazine from my purse to pass the time since it had been over two hours since the doctor had first seen me, then sent me out to wait again.

Of course he went through his series of medical questions. Wanted to know my family history. I told him I had no family. Was left in the world all alone. Dr. Edwards shot me a sympathetic smile before continuing to ask about my symptoms. I told him how many days I'd had a fever, and how I had been nauseous off and on for the past few days. Once again, he shot me another pitiful look.

"You may be pregnant," I remembered him saying casually. "Would that be a good thing for you or bad?"

His comments were unethical, but I knew it was hard for him to remain professional by the way he studied me. He really wanted to know if I had a man. Was I committed was what he wanted to say. And he definitely wanted me. I could feel it. He had been flirting with me from the moment I walked into his examination room.

"I'm not seeing anybody serious, but I've had a relationship or two," I stated.

"Is that so," he commented, moving closer.

"You have a steady boyfriend?"

"Nope, but the job is open." I opened my legs wide, hoping he could see my pussy hairs in between the white paper robe he'd given me.

"We'll see about that." He grinned widely, showing every tooth in his mouth. "My goodness, Chloe, where did you get all those scratches, and bruises on the side of your face? And your neck," he added, clutching my chin.

"Rough sex," I teased. "Doc, I think there's a lump on my breast. Can you check it for me?"

"Chloe, that might not be a good idea in here. There's another time, another place for that." He stopped to watch me fondle my breast. "But this is the time to say, protect yourself in the future," he preached, before telling me I would have to take a pregnancy test, two other tests, and get my blood checked for a rare disease. He said the nurse would come in to do everything. I just remembered nodding to everything he said, considering that he had me hypnotized. Everyone in the office noticed too, I was sure.

Truth be told, the nigga was fine so he could shoot me

as many personal and affectionate looks that he wanted. He was in his mid-thirties, lighter than I liked my men, but had a nice body, and a hell of a practice. I could see myself with him, as long as he made me a kept woman, and in charge of the bitches at the front desk. I was tired of the chasing money scene, and thought about going after a professional man with big money. Legal money.

I knew Dr. Edward's office made crazy money by the number of patients he had, and the fact that we all waited for hours due to the number of people being serviced in the office. I snapped back to the present and got pissed when I saw him walk past the front office, where he laughed along with the head nurse with a thousand micro-braids, and who I hated with a passion.

His eyes darted over in my direction, as he said, "Just a few more minutes, Chloe."

I nodded then added an evil smirk just before zooming in on Tommy's article.

"Just waiting for the results of the last test."

My arms were crossed and my body slumped down in the chair. "No problem, Doc," I said. "Did you just want me to be last, so we can be alone," I added sarcastically.

He knew I was referring to the fact that there were now only two people left in the waiting room with me. But he took my comment in stride. "No, it's not that. We sent your blood down to the lab for testing. We called down and they said they are reviewing the other two tests you took."

I started thinking about the possibility of me being pregnant. The possibility of carrying someone inside of me, then raising the child to call my own. *Damn, that's what my mother did, and fucked my life up*! I thought, stomping the floor.

I wasn't ready. I knew it. I wasn't like Oshyn, the type of person who wanted to make breakfast every morning, comb hair, check homework, and all the other bullshit that comes along with being a mother. I wanted to be a hooker and a housewife all in the same breath.

The thought of Oshyn sent my mind wondering. It was a place that was pleasant for me. The graveyard. The place where all my folk roamed. Word on the street was that Oshyn was really dead. Dead as in six feet under. Streets say she did it herself, at the hotel when she thought she had me. I would've given anything to see it. And killed her a second time if given the chance.

The craziest part of it all was that there was no funeral. I searched high and low, trying to get information about the location of her body, hopefully with one more chance of getting at Bella. The latest reports told me somebody had Oshyn's body shipped to an unknown location to be buried. I wondered who? And why? *We* had no family. *We* had no friends. And she no longer had Brooklyn.

Then my thoughts switched back to Tommy, and the magazine I held in my hand. I started reading the feature, and realized just after two minutes of reading that Tommy was really getting money. It talked about how he was living the good life, while battling health challenges, and missing love in his life. It said he was looking for someone to love, and to share his life, and fortune with.

I got angry.

Threw the magazine across the floor.

Decided I would get up and stomp on it.

But suddenly I was interrupted.

"Ahhh…Ms. Rodriquez, you can come on back," the nurse said.

"Finally," I mumbled, rushing from the waiting area around to where the nurse stood. She had a pencil stuck in between her braids, scratching for dear life.

"Follow me."

"Took you long enough," I belted.

She stopped in the middle of the narrow hallway, causing my body to bump into hers. Turning slowly, she threw her hands on her hips, ready to blast me. "It took a while because the lab workers wanted to double check your results." Her words spat out slowly, and the look on her face was grim.

After watching her expression, I decided to shut up, and just followed her into the room. I could tell she was mad as she pulled a new white covering onto the table, instructing me to leave my clothes on this time. She never gave me eye contact, simply gave off a weird vibe.

"The doctor should be in shortly," she said, slamming the door behind her.

"Fuck that bitch," I belted, while staring at the blank white walls around me. I hopped up on the table, thinking about the outcome of my pregnancy. And thinking about how I would fuck Edwards before we left the room. My bitch-ass nurse told me not to get undressed, but I considered doing it anyway. I wondered what Doc Edwards would say if he walked in and saw me ass naked on his examining table. I laughed to myself, trying to get happy because I figured my news wasn't so great.

I had already come to grips with the fact that I was pregnant. I didn't think I could conceive after how Oshyn tore my insides out with that blade. The stabbing was treacherous, but I had been through worse. A week and a half in the hospital was it. I was tough like that. Like Michelin tires, built to last. So if I was pregnant, I had two choices; hop up on somebody's table and have them vacuum my wound, or become a mother. If I chose the latter, the plan was to get knocked up this month by some paid ass dude, then tell him that the baby is his. I laughed again until I heard the three knocks on the door.

"C'mon in," I said seductively, then threw my right leg over the left.

"Chloe," the doc said, peeping before opening the door all the way.

I sat straight up. "I'm ready to hear. What's up?"

"Soooo," he began uneasily.

Quickly, I changed my mood because his was so damn depressing. He'd done a complete three sixty from the Mr. Bubbly he had portrayed just an hour ago.

"Doc, it can't be that bad. If I'm pregnant we can still be together."

I laughed. He didn't.

"Hey, I was thinking, maybe we could get together tonight." I waited. And waited, hoping for a response. "It's okay," I said, clutching my stomach. "I know you're feeling me, and I'm definitely feeling you. The daddy is long gone."

Doc Edwards pushed his palm toward my face, signaling me to stop. Every sign of joy had been removed from his face.

"Doc, give it to me straight, no chaser."

"Chloe, I sent your blood work down to the lab. You agreed to get tested for HIV, although that's not what I thought you had... but your test results are positive."

I fell back onto the table, attempting to catch my breath. "Did you say positive? As in I got HIV?"

I started breathing hard.

Fast.

Uncontrollably.

"Calm down, Chloe." The doctor took two steps in my direction.

"Calm down? That shit that kills people!" I blurted out. It seemed like my body overheated in just seconds, causing me to pull my hair back for some relief.

"Chloe, understand that you are in the early stages of HIV. You do not have AIDS." He paused, allowing his brows to crinkle. "Not yet anyway."

"Fuck...fuck...fuck!" I shouted, then threw my head back in anguish.

His whole demeanor had changed. His tone wasn't as friendly, and he damn sure wasn't interested in flirting anymore. I watched him closely as he stood three steps away from me writing several notes on my chart. I wanted to ask questions, but was still partially in a state of shock.

"What does this mean?" I snarled, attempting to regain my composure.

A knock sounded at the door, then it opened slowly.

218

The person I didn't want to see stood there with several pamphlets and a clipboard.

"Chloe, my head nurse, Shaniqua, will take it from here. I've got an appointment."

Shaniqua stood in the doorway, unsympathetically waiting for Doctor Edwards to slip behind her. No sooner than he left, she started in on me.

"Okay, not sure if you know, but one of the main causes of HIV is through sexual intercourse. It can enter your body through certain membranes of the anus, vagina or mouth. So, I'm sure you know how you got it." She paused and ran her long fingernail up and down the list on her paper. "Question is…can you get in touch with all your recent sexual partners to notify them?"

The entire time Shaniqua talked, my eyes remained glassy. At one point I could see her lips moving but heard nothing. My life had taken a turn that I never expected.

"HIV," I said to myself slowly.

"Do you hear me, Ms. Rodriquez!"

"Bitch, I hear you!" I shouted back.

The nurse from hell popped her neck backward, wanting to get hood with me. She must've thought about her job, and decided to continue reading from the paper. "Okay, on to the meds. They are pricey, so get ready to spend."

I just sat still, staring off into space.

"There's a wide range to choose from, Emtrivia roughly $350 a month, and then there's Fuzem, that'll run you about $2,500 a month."

"Are you done?" I asked, lifting myself off the table. I showed no emotion.

"Listen, Ms. Rodriquez, this is not a death sentence," she said, sounding as if she cared for the first time. "You just have to take the medication and learn to live with it."

"Yeah. Sure. This is great."

"Listen, this is important," she said to me, after seeing my hand on the door knob. "Make sure you wear a condom so that you don't infect others."

I laughed heartily as if I hadn't just gotten word that I had HIV. I opened the door confidently, telling myself I would get through this. Like I did in every other aspect of my life. I would use this situation to come out on top. No matter what others would say, I would make it work for me.

Then it hit me as I walked back down the narrow hallway, I didn't have to lose my mistress status because of some nagging-ass disease. I laughed heartily. "It wouldn't take control of me," I boasted. "I would take control of it." And every nigga who came in contact with me would get infected. If they paid me well, they could possibly get the memo in a decent amount of time to get treated. Others...well fuck'em. They get what they deserve.

I stopped by the front desk on my way out, only to see Dr. Edwards behind the computer table snuggled up with a nurse. It didn't bother me, he was fair game.

"Hey doc, you sure you don't want to go out tonight?" I stuck my tongue out for added effects. Of course he turned his head. But I walked out of his office as if nothing had changed. Not my attitude, and not my ruthless intentions in life. But indeed, my whole life had changed.

Had places to go.

People to fuck.

And niggas to infect.

Chapter Thirty
(Oshyn)

This was it.

Death.

My spirit effortlessly lifted from my body and floated to the illuminating light that awaited me. It seemed as though my eyes had become immune to the light that once blinded me, as I didn't have to shield them for protection. This time, I was *supposed* to be here. I looked down at my body, which was covered in blood, and was instantly saddened that it all had to end like this.

So tragic.

So alone.

So painful.

But I was tired of all that life had to offer me, and was ready for it all to be over. My whole family had now crossed over to the other side, and I wanted to be with them. This was the only choice I had.

"Mommy!" Micah screamed, as he ran to me. His long and hard embrace let me know that he wasn't mad about me leaving him before, just happy I had returned as promised. I dug my head in his shoulder and whispered, "I'll never leave you again!"

When I lifted my head back up, my mother, Roslyn,

my grandmother, and Apples had all gathered around and waited patiently for their chance to greet me. We had eternity. There was no rush. My best friend, Apples, hadn't changed one bit. Long curl locks, freckled face, and green eyes were still permanent fixtures, and her immorality seemed to have made her even more beautiful than before.

"Thank you for taking care of Bella," she said to me as we hugged. "I watched you the whole time, and I'm grateful that you took her in and loved her like your own."

"But we're family and you would've done the same for me," I said, right before I looked over at Micah. "As a matter of fact, you did do that for me!"

"Welcome home, baby!"

My mother, who had been taken out of my life at the hands of Chloe, was now here with me. We hugged and kissed, cherishing the fact that we were all back together again.

"Where's Mahogany?" I asked.

"She's with Chloe," my mother answered back. I was hoping that I'd see the two of them together, happy again, but I was sure that Chloe needed her mother more.

"Where is my husband? The kids?" I asked everyone, as I looked around.

"What are you talking about?" my mother answered. "There not here."

"But they're supposed to be! Where are they?"

"No, take a look."

My mother pointed down and redirected my attention back to my hotel room. Back to my dead body. Just as I was about to tell her that I didn't see anything, the door opened and Bella walked in, followed by Brooklyn, with our son in one hand and his other hand in a sling. And then they screamed.

I looked on in horror as Brooklyn handed Mye off to Bella and ran over to my cold body to check for a pulse. Then he screamed out my name, and like the pulse confirmed, got no answer.

"He was dead! Brooklyn was murdered! I saw it with my own eyes. He was shot and then died!"

"No. The bullet hit his arm. Main artery. Paramedics came and saved his life before he bled out."

"They are still alive," I screamed to my grandmother. "Why didn't you just tell me that they were still alive?" She never answered my question, just looked away.

"Take me back!"I screamed, no longer wanting to be here. "Take me back!"

"There is no going back, sweetheart. This is where your home is now." My mother grabbed my hand and attempted to pull me closer toward the light. "Don't fight it," she said, noticing my resistance. "This was a choice that you made."

"But I thought that they were here! Let me go!"
But she didn't.

The visual of them crying over my body slowly faded away as I was forced closer to the light. This was now my future and the past had to be left behind.

Epilogue

Four Years Later

Normal.

A word that is often taken for granted. A word that the Rodriquez family would never experience. Four years after they found Oshyn's body in the hotel room, Brooklyn Bella, and Mye remained haunted by her absence. Her widowed husband had her body cremated because he didn't want to put his family through anymore funerals. Brooklyn returned to St. Tropez, along with the urn that held Oshyn's ashes. Strangely, he found solace even though he had no female companionship.

Brooklyn drowned himself into the family life by being a stay at home dad and operating his computer business from home. The million dollar life insurance settlement that he was supposed to get for her death was denied because it was ruled a suicide, but he knew that Oshyn wouldn't want someone else taking care of her children, so he did what he could to make her happy.

At thirty seven, Brooklyn was still handsome, but his soul was gone, just as a chunk of Oshyn's had disappeared each time a family member died. He know understood how her grief held her hostage and only wished that he had been more compassionate before, but now it was too late. It was

225

now his heart that ached desperately and his tears that wouldn't stop falling at night, with no one to console him. He was left with only time to heal his open wounds.

Bella, now fourteen, unwillingly became the woman of the house. Mye Storie looked to her for motherly love, and as much as he aggravated her, she knew that he looked up to her. Their murdered mothers were a common bond that they shared and something Brooklyn would never understand.

Her golden blonde hair now reached the bottom of her bra strap and her bright green eyes seemed to darken as the years progressed. Her body mimicked a grown woman, with breasts that were a full C cup, leaving Brooklyn to fight off the boys that came to visit her often. The attitude that she once carried with Oshyn dwindled away as she assumed more responsibility in the house, but often returned when Brooklyn tried to date women that never met her expectations. She set it in her mind that no one would meet her expectations and anyone he decided to date would have hell to pay. This was the only family that she had left and she was going to make sure that no one can in between that.

On the surface, Bella seemed to be coping with every issue in her young life. But deep down inside she had a vendetta to settle. She vowed that one day she would return to the states, in search of Chloe, to settle the score. The blood feud that had been going on for years was not over as far as she was considered. But Bella remained confident that as soon as she touched U.S. soil, Chloe would be hers.

Chloe and her positive HIV situation seemed like a national catastrophe. Never in a million years did she think that something like the HIV virus was ever going to happen to her. Only bum bitches got the disease was what she thought, but then had a rude awakening. Nine different pills was now what she had for breakfast.

Six more for lunch.

And two for dinner.

Chloe said goodbye to the city of Rochester forever and moved her one woman show to Atlanta, Georgia where no one knew who she was. With her weight back up and her butt implants the size of Nicki Minaj's ass, she was the talk of town, aiming for business and thug men with the most money. And when they didn't have what she was looking for, she still gave them some complimentary pussy.

Atlanta had no idea that the woman that came to take over their city was infecting every man she came in contact with. Her classy business woman look fooled them all as they allowed her to hop on their dicks without a condom. Little did they know that the pleasant surprise they felt at the moment, would be their downfall. But this was her new mission. Miss HIV.

Although she was happy to hear on the news of Oshyn's death, it still saddened her that it wasn't her hands that committed the murder. She knew that Brooklyn and the kids were still alive and made a vow to take care of them once and for all, but with her new mission of using her pussy as a deadly weapon and killing as many men as she could with the virus, she had time to plan her attack.
She had run through over two hundred men since she became a Georgia peach and planned on fucking as many more men as she could until her body gave up.

The dreams she once had of building a family of her own was no longer a priority to her, but rather a forgotten nightmare that she knew would never happen. Her fate would be the same as Oshyn's, death at a young age.
She vowed to be ready for it when it came.

IN STORES NOW   COMING SOON

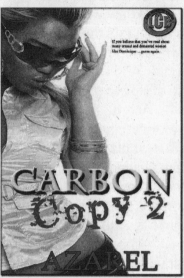

Meet Dominique Lewis, a foul, hard-boiled, go-getter who spends most of her days yearning to be just like her sister, and plotting on taking her man. For her, it's all about money, sex, and power. Although she possesses the perfect physique and sexy features, her life-long dream is to become wealthy and a house-hold name. By any means necessary, she vows to get what she wants.

As Dominique's mission unfolds, she manages to get connected to Yuri, a violent replacement for the man she really sought. After realizing she's partnered with a beast, her world turns upside down. And soon, after the tragic murder of her sister, all hell breaks loose when Dominique's cover is blown.

Armed with revenge on the brain, and a status goal in mind, Dominique soon appoints herself as Rapheal's woman, the most sought after millionaire in Atlanta. Raphael's lavish status in town would put her on a new level, right where she always dreamed...the only problem ...he never said he wanted her. In an effort to hold on to Rapheal, and all the elaborate material possessions, Dominique sets out on a deadly mission to remove anything that stands in her way.

HOT TITLES COMING SOON

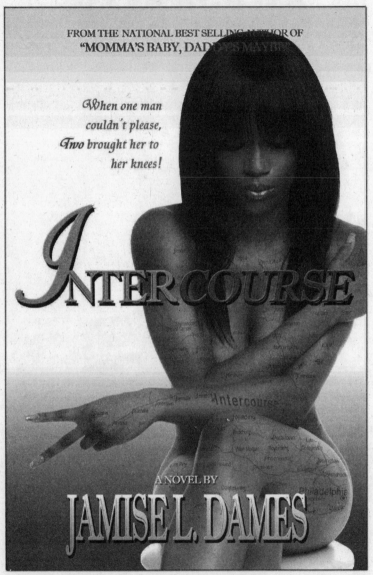